The WATCHER of WAIPUNĀ
and Other Stories

GARY PAK

BAMBOO RIDGE PRESS
1992

This is a special double issue of *Bamboo Ridge, The Hawaii Writers' Quarterly*, issue nos. 55 and 56, ISSN 0733-0308.

ISBN 0-910043-28-0
Library of Congress Catalog Card Number 92-426
Indexed in the American Humanities Index
Copyright 1992 Gary Pak
Most of the stories in this collection were previously published in slightly altered versions in *Bamboo Ridge, Hawai'i Review, Honolulu Magazine, Mānoa* and *Scrawling Wall*.

All Rights reserved by the author. This book, or parts thereof, may not be reproduced in any form without permission of the author. Printed in the United States.
Published by Bamboo Ridge Press.
Editors: Eric Chock, Darrell Lum and Holly Yamada.
Copy Editor: Milton Kimura
Managing Editor: Cathy Song Davenport
Cover and book design: Susanne Yuu
Cover photography: "Nā Koena O Wā Kamali'i Ma Keana" (pier) by Anne Kapualani Landgraf. "Mai'a 'o Kukuiokāne" (bananas) by Mark Hamasaki.
Typesetting: HonBlue Inc.

Bamboo Ridge Press is a non-profit, tax exempt organization formed to foster the appreciation, understanding, and creation of literary, visual, audio-visual and performing arts by and about Hawaii's people. Your tax-deductible contributions are welcomed.

Bamboo Ridge Press is supported in part by grants from the State Foundation on Culture and the Arts (SFCA). The SFCA is funded by appropriations from the Hawaii State Legislature and by grants from the National Endowment for the Arts. This book is also supported in part by a grant from the National Endowment for the Arts (NEA), a federal agency.

Bamboo Ridge Press is member of the Council of Literary Magazines and Presses (CLMP).

Subscriptions to *Bamboo Ridge, The Hawaii Writers' Quarterly* are available for $16/year.

Bamboo Ridge Press
P.O. Box 61781
Honolulu, Hawaii 96839-1781

10 9 8 7 6 5 4 3 2   95 96

Library of Congress Cataloging-in-Publication Data

Pak, Gary, 1952–
    The Watcher of Waipuna and other stories / by Gary Pak.
      p. cm. -- (Bamboo Ridge ; no. 55-56)
    ISBN 0-910043-28-0 (pbk.) : $8.00
    1. Hawaii--Fiction. I. Title. II. Series.
PS3566.A39W37 1992
813'.54--dc20   92-426
                                              CIP

ACKNOWLEDGEMENTS

I wish to give my thanks to the members of the Study Group and the editors of Bamboo Ridge Press—Eric Chock, Darrell Lum, Holly Yamada, Milton Kimura and Cathy Song—for their camaraderie and invaluable insights. A special thanks to Susanne Yuu for designing the book. I also wish to thank the following people for their generous friendships: Wing Tek Lum, Bob Onopa and Rob Wilson. And a toast to my brothers on the road: Ron, Ed, Ralph and Eugene.

I wish to thank my family for their everlasting love and sustenance: to my grandparents (both sides); to my parents; to all of my aunties and uncles and cousins; to my parents-in-law; and, of course, to my wife and children.

Finally, I wish to thank the Ludwig Vogelstein Foundation of Brooklyn, New York, for its generous support.

TO MOM AND DAD

TABLE *of* CONTENTS

9 The VALLEY *of the* DEAD AIR

21 The WATCHER *of* WAIPUNA

87 *For the* SAKE *of a* CHRIST

95 The TRIAL *of* GORO FUKUSHIMA

113 A TOAST *to* ROSITA

127 *The* GIFT

155 *An* OLD FRIEND

167 *The* GARDEN *of* JIRO TANAKA

179 ABOUT *the* AUTHOR

The VALLEY of the DEAD AIR

The day after Jacob Hookano died, that old hermit who had lived at the very end of Waiola Valley, a bad air from the ocean came in and lingered over the land. The residents of the valley thought that a Kona wind had brought in that rotten smell from the mangroves and mud flats of the coastal area, and they waited impatiently for another wind to take the smell away.

As Leimomi Vargas said succinctly, "Jus' like old Jacob wen fut and dah fut jus' stayin' around."

And stay around it did, for weeks. There seemed no end. The residents prayed for that new wind to blow the obstinate smell away, but no wind came and the air became stagnant and more foul as if the valley were next to an ancient cesspool that had suddenly ruptured after centuries of accumulations. The malodor permeated the wood of the houses, it tainted the fresh clothes hung to dry, and it entered the pores of everyone, making young and old smell bad even after a good scrubbing. The love lives of the residents became nonexistent.

"We gotta do somet'ing 'bout dis hauna," Joseph Correa complained. The retired sewers worker from the City and County sat on a chair under the eaves of an old abandoned store that fronted the main road.

"Yeah, but what?" said Bobby Ignacio. He turned his gaunt, expressionless face towards Correa, then returned to his meditation of birds eating the ripened fruits of a lichee tree across the road.

"You know, Bobby," Correa said in a voice shaded ominously, "I betchu dah gov'ment is behind all dis. Look how long dis hauna stay heah. Long time already. If was jus' one nat'ral t'ing, dah wind already blow 'em away."

Ignacio, a truck farmer up the road in the valley, spat disconsolately into the wild grass growing on the side of the store.

"But I tell you dis, Bobby. I betchu one day dah gov'ment goin' come down heah and dey goin' brag how dey can take dis hauna away. And den they *goin'* take 'em away. But I betchu little while aftah dat, dey goin' come back and try ask us for do dem one favor. You watch." Correa nodded his head. "No miss."

The farmer shrugged his narrow shoulders. "But you know what everybody saying?"

"Who everybody?"

"Everybody."

"So what everybody saying?"

"Dey saying old Jacob dah one doing all dis."

The old retiree nervously stretched out his tired legs, his head twitched a few times, then he looked out languidly towards the mango trees across the road.

"I nevah had no problems with old Jacob," Correa said weakly. "I was always good to him. I nevah talk stink 'bout him or anything li' dat."

The smell persisted, and somehow it infected the rich, famous soil of the valley. The earth began to emit a terrible odor of rotten fish. While plowing one corner of his sweet potato field, Tats Sugimura uncovered a hole full of fish scales and fish bones. He didn't think anything of it until his wife complained to him later how fishy everything smelled. The bad smell of the valley had numbed his nose so Tats couldn't smell anything worth shit now. His wife, on the other hand, had a super-sensitive nose and she often would sniff the air in her kitchen and know exactly what the Rodriguez family was cooking a quarter of a mile down the road.

"Tats, you wen dump some rotten fish around here or what?" she said. Sugimura shook his head. He wasn't the talking type, even with his wife. "Den whas dat stink smell?"

He thought of telling her about the fish scales and bones, then he thought that perhaps a bunch of stray cats had had a feast in that corner of his field. The fish were probably tilapia or catfish the cats had caught in the nearby stream. But he was tired from working all day under the hot sun and in the stifling humid air and he didn't have the energy to describe to his wife what he had seen. The fish scales and fish bones were unimportant, and he shrugged his thin, wiry shoulders and said nothing.

But something bad was in the soil. When Tats and the other sweet potato farmers began harvesting their produce a few days later, they found abnormally small sweet potatoes, some having the peculiar shape of a penis.

"How dah hell we goin' sell dis kine produce?" complained Earl Fritzhugh, a part-Hawaiian sweet potato farmer. "Dey goin' laugh at us. So small. And look at dis one. Look like one prick!"

"Somet'ing strange goin' on in dis valley," said Darryl Mineda, another farmer. "Get dah story goin' around dat old Jacob doin' all dis to get back."

"Get back at who?" Fritzhugh asked irately.

"At us."

Fritzhugh looked at Mineda incredulously. "At us? Why dat old Hawaiian like get back at us fo'? He wen live by himself. Nobody wen bother him."

Mineda shook his head. "Somebody tol' me all dah land in dis valley used to be his family's land, long time ago. Den dah Cox family wen come in and take dah land away from his family. Somet'ing 'bout Jacob's family not paying dah land tax or water tax or somet'ing li' dat, and dah haole wen pay instead."

"But what got to do with us? I not responsible. Dah haole wen do it. Not me."

Mineda shrugged his shoulders.

"Eh, I was good to dah old man," Fritzhugh said. "I nevah bother him. When he used to go up and down dis road, he nevah said not'ing to me, so I never say not'ing to him." He paused. "But I wonder who goin' get his land now he ma-ke. He no mo' children, eh?"

Mineda shrugged his shoulders again. "Maybe das why," Mineda said.

"Maybe das why what?"

"Maybe das why he got all salty. Nobody pay attention to him. Nobody talk story with him. Nobody go bother him."

"So what you goin' do? Dah buggah dead already."

"What . . . you no believe in dah spirits?"

"Eh, no fut around."

"No. I asking you one simple question. You believe in dah kine Hawaiian spirits or what?"

"Yeah, I believe in dat kine," Fritzhugh said, looking warily across his sweet potato field, then back to Mineda's furrowed face. "But so what? Why . . . you think he wen curse dah valley or what?"

Mineda looked at this feet. He was silent for a while. "Crazy," he said finally. "All of dis. And how we going sell our produce to dah markets?"

A white car with the state emblem on the doors came by the store one day. Correa sat up and stared into the car curiously. Then he nodded his head. "You see, Bobby, you see," he said. "What I tol' you. Dah gov'ment goin' come down heah and try get somet'ing from us. I tol' you all along, dis hauna was from dah gov'ment. What I tol' you?"

Ignacio leaned forward, squinting his eyes to read the emblem. "Department of Agriculture," he muttered. He slouched back into his seat.

"What I tol' you, eh, Bobby? Look, dah Japanee going come out and he goin' try smooth talk us. You watch."

"Fritzhugh wen call dem fo' come down and try figure out whas wrong with dah dirt."

"Look dah buggah, nice clean cah, air conditionah and everyt'ing," Correa said sardonically, pretending he had not heard what his friend had said.

The man got out of the car and went up to the two men.

"Yes, sir," Correa said officiously. "What can I do fo' you today?"

The man crimped his nose at the fetid air. "You know where I can find Earl Fritzhugh?"

"Yeah-yeah. He live up dah valley. Whas dis fo'?" Correa asked.

"He called me about some problems you farmers having over here. Something about the soil."

"Not dah soil," Correa said. "Dah air. You cannot smell how hauna dah air is?"

The man nodded his head. "Yes . . . yes, the air kind of stink. Smell like rotten fish."

"Smell like somebody wen unload one big pile shit in dah middle of dah valley."

The man from the state grinned.

"So why you come," Correa asked pointedly, "and not one guy from dah Department of Air?"

The man from the state looked at Correa with dying interest. "You can tell me where Earl Fritzhugh lives?" he asked Ignacio.

"Yeah, brah," Ignacio said, pointing up the valley road. "You go up this road, maybe one mile into the valley. You goin' pass one big grove bamboo on the right side. The farm right after that going be the Fritzhugh farm. No can miss 'em."

The man thanked him, then got back into the car and left.

"You better call up Fritzhugh and tell him dah Japanee comin' up question him," Correa said.

Ignacio waved the flies away from his face, then spat into the grass.

There was nothing wrong with the soil, the state worker told them a few days after he had come up and taken samples to the downtown laboratory. Nothing was wrong. The farmers left that meeting with remorse. Then what was wrong with the crops?

A day later heavy rains came, and for three days the whole valley was inundated with torrents and flash floods. The residents welcomed the storm, for they believed that the rains would wash the soil of the inscrutable poison and cleanse the air of the bad smell. But came the fourth day and a bright sun and when the residents smelled the air again, the odor was still there, now more pronounced than ever and denser. It was as if the storm had nurtured the smell like water nourishes plants.

"You did anyt'ing to old Jacob?" people were now asking each other. And the answer was always, "No . . . but did you?" And when the informal polling was completed, it was determined that everybody in the valley had left old Jacob alone. But they all cast accusing looks at one another, as if everyone else but themselves were responsible for the curse that old Jacob seemed to have thrown over the once peaceful and productive valley.

One morning a haole salesman came to the doorsteps of one of the houses.

"Heard you folks here were having problems with fires," he said in a jovial voice, a Mid-Western accent.

"No," Tats Sugimura's wife said sourly. "Not fires. The smell. You cannot smell dah stink smell?"

The haole laughed. "Well, you know what they say," he said.

"No, what dey say?" Harriet said.

"They say that if you can't see it, then you can surely smell it." He laughed again. Harriet was about to ask who had said that when the salesman segued quickly into a sales pitch about a new fire prevention system his company was now offering in the area. And, for a limited time, he concluded, they would install the entire system without charge.

"We not interested," Harriet Sugimura said. "Go away. Go talk to somebody else."

"But you don't understand," the salesman said. "Along with this fire prevention system comes our new, revolutionary, home-odors maintenance system. And for a limited time, we will give it to you free if you purchase our fire prevention system. Here . . . smell this."

The salesman took out a small aerosol can and sprayed it inside the Sugimuras' house from the front door. Instantly, the spray cleared the air of the ugly smell that Harriet had almost gotten used to and the whole living room smelled fresh like roses.

"Your system can do this?" she gasped with delight.

"Yes, and more. Why, because our system is computer-controlled, you don't have to lift a finger. Everything will be done automatically."

Harriet's face beamed with promise. It had been so long since she smelled the scent of flowers. "So how much is it?"

"Retail, it sells for eight-hundred and fifty dollars. But for this limited offer, we will sell it to you for two-hundred and fifty dollars."

"Two-hundred-fifty!"

"Well, if you know of a friend or neighbor or family who would want this system too, I can give it to you for two-twenty-five."

"Hmm. Wait, let me call my neighbor."

Soon, the entire valley was buzzing on the telephone lines talking about that new machine that would wipe out the bad smell in the homes. If the valley was going to stay bad smelling, that didn't mean the homes had to have that smell, too. So almost every other household bought one of those systems, and the salesman, being a nice guy, even reduced the price by another twenty-five dollars, prepayment, stating emphatically that the company was now making only a twenty-dollar profit from each unit sold. The residents waited impatiently for that big brown truck that the haole promised would bring the fire-prevention-home-odor-maintenance system, and they waited past the promised three days delivery period, but the truck never came.

The smell worsened to the point that every other person in the valley was getting a constant headache.

"Somet'ing has to be done about the smell," Ignacio said. "If we cannot do anyt'ing about it, den we gotta take dis to the state."

"Nah, how you can do dat?" Correa said. "Dah state already wen say dey cannot do not'ing about it."

"But something gotta be done," Ignacio said.

"Something gotta be done," Harriet Sugimura said to her husband, sheepishly, a few days after her husband, for the first time in seven years, had lost his temper when she told him how she had spent their tax refunds.

"If this smell continue on, I'm getting the hell out of this valley," Pat Fritzhugh said to her husband.
"Me, too," Fritzhugh replied.

"You know what the problem is?" Leimomi Vargas said to her neighbor, Elizabeth Kauhale. "The problem is nobody honest wit' everybody else. I betchu somebody wen get the old man real angry. Really angry. And das why he wen curse the valley wit' dis stink fut smell before he ma-ke."

"I think you right, Lei," Elizabeth said sadly. "We gotta be honest wit' each other. Das dah only way."

"Then maybe the old man going take back the curse," Lei said.

"Maybe we should go get one kahuna bless dah friggin', stinkin' place," Elizabeth said.

"You nevah know the old man was one kahuna?"

"I know, but he dead."

"Still yet."

"But I t'ink you right. We gotta get to the bottom of this. Find all the persons responsible for him cursing the valley. Then make them offer somet'ing to the old man's spirit. Or somet'ing like that. Whachu t'ink?"

So from that conversation, the two women went door to door, struggling with the others to be honest. For starts, Lei told about the time when she was a small girl and she went up to the old man's place and stole an egg from one of his hens. And Elizabeth said one time she saw her brother throw a rock at the old man as he was climbing the road to his hermitage, and because her brother was now living on the Big Island, she would take responsibility for his wrong action. Then, slowly, the others began to unfold their stories of wrongdoings against the old man, even Joseph Correa, who admitted that he wronged old Jacob when they were young men growing up in the valley and wooing the same girl and he had told her parents that Jacob didn't have a prick and that he was a mahu. About the only person who hadn't sinned against Jacob was Tats Sugimura, who lived the next lot down from Jacob's. In fact, he had been kind to Jacob, giving him sweet potatoes and letting him use his water at the far end of the field (where Tats had found the fish scales and bones, though Tats couldn't figure out that that was where Jacob used to clean his fish).

So they organized representatives from each household of the valley to go up the road and pay their homage to Jacob's vindictive soul. They went to his place one late Saturday afternoon when the sun was beginning to set behind the mountains, parking their cars and trucks at the end of the dirt road where the road turned into a trail that led into Jacob's forbidden plot of land. They brought taro, sweet potatoes, corn, watermelons, yams, several 'awa roots, a dozen cans of meat, a basket of freshly laid eggs, a tub of fish and another tub of crawling crabs, loads of ti leaves, bunches of green bananas, and a fifth of good bourbon so that Jacob could wash all of the offerings down. They silently climbed the narrow path that the valley road turned into, winding up through dense brush and trees towards old Jacob's place. Lei was the only one in the contingent who had been up to Jacob's place before, but that was years and years ago and all she had seen were the dilapidated chicken coops, and everyone's senses were suspended in fear, not knowing what they might expect or see at the end of the trail.

Finally, they reached a flat clearing where they saw a sweeping view of the precipitous mountain range. They searched anxiously for his house until finally Elizabeth Kauhale found it hanging a few feet above the ground, with vines attaching it to a giant kukui tree. It was made out of scrap wood and looked like a big crate with a small opening on the side where a tattered rope ladder hung down. The box house began to swing and there was heard hollow laughter coming from within. The entourage retreated a few steps, their faces blanched with the expectation that Jacob's ghost might leap out after them. The laughing stopped, and they quickly dropped their offerings in an untidy heap under Jacob's pendular house, not daring to glance up the rope ladder. Then, hurriedly, they filed down the trail.

When they reached the bottom, they stopped, looked back, and made sure everyone who had gone up was back down. After they finished counting heads, they ambled off to their cars, murmuring among themselves how they hoped things would come out all right and the smell would leave the valley. Then, suddenly, there came loud, crackling laughter from deep in the valley that made the plants and trees shake. Everyone crammed into whosesoever's car was nearest. They raced down the road and did not stop until, breathless and terrified and worried for their very lives, they were down at the old abandoned store, and here they sat speechless until Leimomi Vargas shouted at the top of her lungs, "I think dis is all silly—us guys getting our pants scared off our 'okoles!"

Embarrassed smiles came upon everyone's face and there was heard some nervous laughter. Someone suggested that they celebrate in the memory of old Jacob, and, without further ado, they voted unanimously to go back to their homes and get what they had to eat and bring it all back down to the abandoned store where they would party for the rest of the night. So the people who were in the wrong cars got out and into the cars they had originally gone up the road with, and they all went back home and took boxes of chicken or beef or squid or whatever they had out of the freezers and thawed them under warm running water; the Ignacios brought down a pig Bobby had slaughtered that morning; the Fritzhughs brought a big barrel of fish their oldest son had caught that day; and Tats Sugimura trucked down a load of his miniature, mutant sweet potatoes; and the others went into backyards and lopped off hands of bananas and picked ears of corn and mangoes and carried off watermelons from the fields; and they brought all that food and all the beer and whiskey they had in their homes down to the store. Earl Fritzhugh and his two sons chopped up a large kiawe tree and made a roaring fire in the empty lot next to the store, and everyone pitched in and cooked the copious amounts of food in that sweet-smelling, charcoal inferno. Bobby Ignacio and friends—Earl Fritzhugh, Fritzhugh's youngest son, Sonny Pico's two boys and his daughter, Tats Sugimura's brother and Joseph Correa—brought down their ukes and guitars and a washtub bass and provided the entertainment that lasted exactly three nights and two days. And when the festivities finally ended—the smoke from the kiawe fire was still smoldering strongly—everyone at the old store began hugging each other and then meandered off to their homes.

But before they fell into deep sleep, Earl Fritzhugh and his wife made love for the first time since the smell began putrefying the air of the valley. And so did Tats and Harriet Sugimura. And there were at least a dozen or so illegitimate liaisons committed that festive time—for one, Elizabeth Kauhale saw her teenage son go in the bush with Bobby Ignacio's willowy daughter—which was probably the reason why weeks ahead there would be more festivities when three of those liaisons would be legitimized, and why months later, on the same day, there would be added three new members to the community.

And before he slept, old Joseph Correa dragged his feet to the old cemetery next to the clapboard Catholic church, and there he laid a bunch of wild orchids on the grave of his beloved wife, Martha, and he sat down on the soft, wet ground, though it was a struggle for his brittle old legs to do so, and he sang that song that was a favorite of his wife—"Pua Lilia"—because his wife's middle name was Lilia, and he had often sung that song to her when she was alive and he had sung that song to her when she was dying. And after that song, he gazed up the valley and apologized once again to his former friend, Jacob Hookano, for saying those damaging things about him in the past. "But she was worth fighting for," he said with a choke in his voice. "And you can see, my friend," he added with a touch of jealousy, "that you with her right now."

When the people of the valley finally woke up the next morning, or the next afternoon—or whenever—the first thing they noticed was the smell. The fresh clean smell of the ocean. It was the smell of salt, and the warm winds that carried it over the valley swept up to the highest ridges of the mountains, and there the warm air married with the cold dampness and thick clouds formed, and soon, with the shift in the trades, rain began to fall over the silent, peaceful valley.

The WATCHER of WAIPUNA

ONE

Gilbert Sanchez didn't know it, but he was going crazy.

Everyone in the village of Waipuna knew about it, even old man Nakakura, who was himself half-crazy, talking all day long about the frogmen who had come to Waipuna from the ocean during the War and were now hiding in the dense mangrove forest along the coast, some forty-plus years after the Big Surrender. Gilbert's older sisters, Lola Makanihi and Lucy Bitten, had known of Gilbert's problem for a while now, since the time Gilbert had given up his job driving the school bus up and down the coast, a job he had performed meticulously for the past seven years since coming home from duty in Nam. Gilbert said that he had quit the job so that he could stay home and take care of his invalid parents.

But everyone in Waipuna knew that that was just an excuse, for they knew that he had quit driving because his fiancée of eleven years, Tricia Kobashigawa, had left him: she had run off with a haole GI whom she met at a bar in Kanewai town where she worked as a waitress. Gilbert was devastated when he heard Tricia had run off with the haole. He had cried all night and into the next morning, debating whether to kill the haole or himself. The next morning was the first time he had ever been late to work; for the children who rode the bus, it was the first time in twelve years that anyone had been tardy.

Late the following afternoon, Gilbert took out his Winchester .30-.06, cleaned and oiled it, then loaded it with one round and stuck the tip of the barrel into his mouth. At the last moment, his incontinent father called him with urgency. Gilbert lowered the rifle, wiped the moisture from his eyes, and went to check on his father, who had done it in his pants. Complaining to himself, he cleaned his father, then himself, then prepared a bland dinner for his parents consisting of potato soup and puréed vegetables. Later that evening, he buried the rifle in a shallow grave on the beach, chiding himself for thinking up such desperate and mindless thoughts: if he had killed the haole, he'd go to jail, leaving his parents defenseless; if he killed himself, he'd go to hell for leaving his parents by themselves. It was a no-win situation. Along with the rifle, Gilbert ceremoniously buried his love for alcohol, pouring out a half-full fifth of Southern Comfort and a half case of Oly, dropping the empty cans and bottle into the pit then filling it with the shovelling of his feet.

Another change eventually came over him.

He began to talk to himself, which was all the reason his sisters needed to conclude that he was a bit "off." (Actually, talking to himself was more of a habit than a sickness, something that he had picked up since it went along fine with the loneliness that came with living at the very end of the Waipuna Coast Road. Though he was in the constant company of his parents, they could say nothing but make aphasic grunts and growls. He needed to talk with someone to break the predominance of silence since the departure of Miss Trish, and the only person around that could provide the necessary return chatter was none other than himself.) This habit became so ingrained that it was natural for Gilbert to talk to himself while in the company of others. So sophisticated became his conversations with himself that he was able to carry out discussions between four Gilberts at the same time, each Gilbert with an absolutely different personality.

This habit disturbed his two sisters. It embarrassed them. But since Gilbert lived at their parents' home which was a good walking distance from the village and hardly came in to socialize, the sisters made a pledge to themselves—in the interest of their family's welfare and reputation—to keep Gilbert's condition a secret, to keep this particular, embarrassing affair of the family as far away from Waipuna's public eye as possible.

It was a pledge that was short-lived, for swiftly developing were events that would cause it to be fast forgotten.

After a round of golf at the prestigious Hawaii Loa Country Club in Town, after a sumptuous dinner of roast suckling pig and lobster, and after an evening with beautiful Suzanne, Nicole, Michelle and Miranda—all who had no last names—four businessmen from Japan and two businessmen from Town struck an agreement to be co-developers of a world-class hotel resort at the isolated tip of Waipuna where seventy-six acres of undeveloped land had been purchased by Hawaiian International Corporation, the parent company of the Honolulu businessmen, thirteen years ago for a song. The only thing preventing the start of the project was the acquisition of a choice beach-front parcel that was in the center of their plans, that piece of land on which the Sanchezes' three-bedroom, weather-beaten, corrugated-roof shack was solidly settled.

Later that week, two black limousines came into Waipuna, carrying the six businessmen, who were distributed evenly racially between the two cars and were now joint owners of the property just mauka of the Sanchezes' five acres of beach-front land. They came to Waipuna to offer the Sanchezes a hundred fifty thousand dollars for each acre of their land; in all, three quarters of a million dollars.

The blazing black caravan wound its way down the coast, which was interspersed with pockets of sandy beach and mangroves, to the Sanchezes' quiet homestead, where a immaculate sandy beach (which locals secretly claimed as the best on the island for diving and shoreline fishing) began and went on uninterrupted for three miles until ended by a black precipice. The limousines slowed at the unmarked, rusty mailbox—unused for 23 years—then turned inland, proceeding up a meandering sandy and grassy road to the house. Behind the spread of kiawe trees rose a magnificent mountain range.

Splitting the faded and tattered kitchen curtains, Gilbert observed the cars coming towards the house. He went out of the house grinning uneasily. Never had he seen a caravan of big cars come all this way just to deliver the weekly groceries. Nakakura's Store must be doing good, he concluded to himself, or they must be crazy. And when the limousines came to a stop and the businessmen got out—the Japanese businessmen coming up to him and shaking his hand, smiling and bowing their heads respectfully—Gilbert was mildly confused. One of the Japanese nationals who was much younger and taller than his companions identified himself as Takemoto and introduced his countrymen, his accent moderately strong but his enunciation well formed and precise. But with his stomach growling, Gilbert was forced to cut through the enigma, asking, "So where dah food?"

The haole businessmen traded grins.

"Hello. My name is Henry Wilkins," one of them said, reaching out to shake Gilbert's hand. "And this is my business associate, Jerris Neuhauser." Gilbert shook hands with the other haole who was taller and thinner. "We're with Hawaiian International Corporation. We're co-owners, with these gentlemen from Japan, of the property right behind this house. We would like to meet with the owner of this property. Are you the owner?"

"Oh, you like see my father, but he sick now. But you can talk to me. But where dah food we wen order? I kinda hungry, and my faddah and muddah . . . dey hungry, too."

"The food?"

"Yeah. You delivering somet'ing fo' us, right?"

"Well . . . yes, in a way," said the other haole. "We're here to 'deliver,' so to speak, an offer for your property. May we come in and talk?"

"We can talk right heah. My folks, dey sleeping right now."

"Sure. That's fine with us." The taller haole looked to his partners, who nodded in approval. He set a briefcase on the hood of the car and opened it, taking out a legal-size folder.

Gilbert eyed the contents of the briefcase and became worried that perhaps the wrong delivery service was sent to them. But he took a longing look at one of the limousines and decided to wait as patiently as possible, for the two cars were big enough to probably contain the entire inventory on the Nakakura's shelves.

"You just gotta cool it little bit," Gilbert scolded his stomach. "No get so impatient or else you going get nothin'."

"Excuse me?" asked Neuhauser.

"Huh? Oh, sometimes I gotta talk sense to him. He trying to control my life. You know what I mean?"

Neuhauser nodded his head, then gave a strange look to Wilkins.

"But I hungry!" Gilbert's stomach cried.

"Shaddup and be patient," Gilbert whispered, away from the ears of his guests. "You disturbing me."

The Japanese nationals, who obviously were letting the haoles talk for them, were smiling uncomfortably. Takemoto whispered something to Wilkins, who whispered something to Neuhauser.

"So what you was saying, then?" Gilbert asked.

"Well, perhaps we can set up a meeting with the appropriate parties involved," Neuhauser suggested. "May we speak to Mr. Gilbert Sanchez, the owner of this property?"

"Oh, but das my father and me."

"I don't understand. On your property deed the registered owner is a Mr. Gilbert Sanchez."

"Das right. Das me and my father. His name is Gilbert and so is mines."

"Oh."

"So what you had in mind about our property?"

"Well, we would like to sit down with . . . you, and see if we can work out an arrangement for the Hawaiian International's use of your property. We're willing to compensate you well for it."

"What you mean?"

"What Jerris is trying to say," Wilkins intervened, "is that Hawaiian International Corporation and the Tokyo Imperial Bank," glancing at Takemoto and friends, "would like to make an offer to buy your property."

"Oh, you like buy our land. How much you like offer?"

"Oh, that would have to take sitting down with you and your family negotiating."

"Yeah, but how much?" Gilbert asked, irritated at the tugging of his stomach.

"Well, I suppose . . . perhaps we may be willing to offer to buy your entire holdings for a hundred fifty thousand dollars an acre. Which, might I add, is way over the market value of land in a rural area like Waipuna."

Gilbert studied the faces of the businessmen, then said, "Oh . . . das too much to spend fo' one piece land."

Thinking that Gilbert was playing the hard negotiator—which he wasn't—the haole businessmen smiled. Wilkins chuckled. Takemoto cleared his throat and said something in Japanese to his fellow countrymen, who either smiled or chuckled. Then Wilkins asked Gilbert about the weather, the problems with being isolated from the rest of the island, and the validity to the claim that the beach was the best on the island. Then they excused themselves with handshakes and goodbyes. They entered the limousines and headed back to their hotels in Town.

When the real delivery boy arrived with the groceries, Gilbert told him what had happened. Soon, all the people up and down the Waipuna coast were buzzing about the great fortune the Sanchez family was about to harvest.

The news hit Lola exactly 37 minutes after the delivery boy returned to Nakakura's Store. Immediately she phoned her sister.

"Tell me one fact," Lola said. "Under whose name Daddy's and Mommy's property stay listed under?"

"I dunno," Lucy answered. "I think maybe Gilbert."

"Gilbert? How dah hell he got his name on dah property deed?"

"Why you asking me fo'?"

TWO

It didn't take long for the two sisters to devise a plan that would get their fingers into that suddenly juicy pie. They decided to talk their parents into scratching Gilbert's name off the deed to the property and inserting their names instead. They would argue that Gilbert was going pupule—if he wasn't totally already—and that he was ready to sell the land to the developers, thus denying their parents their home of over fifty years.

That afternoon the sisters visited their parents. They presented their weepful case, while Gilbert laughed in another room, watching his favorite television game show. Luckily for Gilbert, his parents—their parents—were far too gone mentally to be moved by any emotion. In their present state of mind, they did not understand what was being said or care what was going to happen to them. Their only wish—and it was more of an instinct—was that they die peacefully and soon. Or just soon. Which they did. Mr. Sanchez died three days after the visit, followed a week later by his beloved wife.

"What we going do now?" Lucy asked her sister, two days after their mother's funeral. They were drinking coffee and watching the soaps on a new 13-inch color television in Lucy's kitchen.

"Sammy!" Lola screamed, glaring at her only son, who was watching the air bubbles float lazily to the bottom of an upside-down jar of raw honey. "Stop touching dah honey jar or you going drop 'em and broke 'em on dah floor! I tol' you no touch Auntie Lucy's things! Go watch dah tv and no fool around." She looked at Lucy. "What you said?"

"I said what we going do now, now dat Mama and Daddy not here anymo.'"

That's right! Drive in with any trade-in and we'll guarantee...

"Dat Gilbert! Ovah my dead body I going let him take everything!"

"I heard they wen offer quarter million fo' each acre."

"Where you heard dat from?"

So come on down and join the celebration...

"I heard 'em from Harriet Nakakura."

"You going believe her? She lolo jus' like her old man."

Lucy shrugged her shoulders, then sipped her coffee.

Have you been a victim of an accident that has left...

"Quarter million dollars," Lola murmured. "Dey gotta be kidding. Eh, we gotta get Gilbert unsign his name from the deed. No get me wrong, Lucy. I love my brother just like how you love him."

Have you been wrongfully...

Lucy nodded her head.

"But our brother," Lola continued, "you know our brother. He not in his right frame of mind."

Lucy agreed, then asked what could they do about the situation.

Call us for a . . .

Lola's eyes lingered on a crucifix hung over the kitchen doorway. "Tomorrow we go into Honolulu," she said with deliberation, "and we go see ourselves one good lawyer."

THREE

Gilbert was counting the empty soda bottles in the back of the garage, mainly the collection of his recently deceased father. He would get five cents for each unbroken bottle he deposited at Nakakura's Store. He counted 27 when Charlie the mailman came trundling up the driveway in his delivery car, which surprised Gilbert for the post office had stopped delivering the mail to the Sanchez residence for 23 years; the mail was usually tucked in one of the grocery sacks, which the boy delivered every Thursday morning.

Charlie got out of the government car, took a handkerchief from his back pocket and wiped his forehead.

"Charlie, whachu doing ovah here?"

"How you doing, Gilbert? You been keeping yo'self busy?"

"Jus' cleaning up, little bit. My faddah said he wanted me clean up in the back."

Charlie was going to remind Gilbert that his father had died three months ago but decided not to mention it.

"I got mail fo' you, Gilbert. One registered letter. Must be kinda important. Das why I had to come out all the way here and deliver 'em to you."

"One what?"

"One registered letter. From townside." Charlie held the letter at arm's length, squinted his bushy-eyebrowed eyes and read, "'James Fogarty, Attorney-at-Law.' You know one James Fogarty, Gilbert, one lawyer?"

"No. Whas dat fo'?"

Charlie shook his head. "I dunno, Gilbert. You gotta read 'em fo' find out yo'self. Here, sign right here."

Gilbert took the pen offered by Charlie and placed an "x" on the line. "Charlie, you go read 'em to me. You know I no can read."

Charlie nodded his head knowingly, opened the letter and read it.

Gilbert listened without digesting a sentence. "So what all dat means, Charlie?"

"Dey like you come into town fo' one meeting."

"Who dey?"

"I dunno." Charlie returned the letter to the envelope. "But what I heard, Gilbert, is dat yo' two sistahs behind all dis."

"My sistahs . . . behind what?"

Charlie gave the letter to Gilbert. "Gilbert, you wanna know some advice?"

"Whas dat, Charlie?"

"Watch out yo' sistahs. Dey like take away something dat belong to you."

"My sistahs? Nah. Dey no like not'ing from me."

"Take my word, Gilbert. Blood is thicker than water. But money make the blood thin. Watch out yo' sistahs, Gilbert. They going try do something bad to you."

A tinge of anger shaded Gilbert's eyes; he was the protective type, especially when it came to his family. "Dey my family, Charlie. Family not going make trouble wit' family. Right, Charlie?"

Charlie shrugged his shoulders. He waved a languid good-bye, then got back into the car and drove off.

FOUR

"You think Gilbert going figure something out?" Lucy asked her sister.

They had left the family cemetery that was located in the back end of the Sanchez property, having brought flowers and having offered prayers for their beloved parents. From the dirt path they were on, Lola peered down at the weather-beaten family house: there was no sign of Gilbert anywhere.

"Nah," Lola answered with assurance. "Gilbert so dumb. He think we doing him one favor we tell him we like be his power-of-attorney."

"Try explain that to me . . . power-of-attorney."

"No worry. I understand what the lawyer wen say. In other words, we going get control of Mama's and Papa's estate. Das what counts . . . right?"

Lucy was slow to the answer: "Right."

As they approached the house, Lola spotted Gilbert strolling up the driveway.

"Remember, no tell him anything now," she warned.

Gilbert was carrying a fishing pole, a red scoop net and a plastic bucket that was weighed with something. When he noticed his sisters, a smile on his now-bearded face became wide, and he quickened his steps, splashing water on his rolled-up khaki pants. "Lucy! Lola!" he called. "Long time no see! And then . . . how you folks?"

The sisters smiled weakly.

"Oh—everything all right," Lola said. "And then . . . how you?"

"Oh, I okay." He set his fishing equipment down and hugged his sisters generously. "I nevah see you people long time. So what brings you here? Come—we go inside and talk story."

"We came here put flowers on Mama's and Papa's grave, Gilbert. We gotta go back already." Lola cast a longing eye at her old Chevy truck that was parked in the front of the house, hoping to give Lucy a clue as to what was on her mind. "Maybe next time, Gilbert, maybe next time we can stay little longer."

"Ahhh . . . come inside fo' little while. I like show you what I did to the house."

"No, Gilbert," Lucy said. "We haf' to go already. Uh . . . gotta pick up the children from school."

Gilbert glanced at the sun. "So early?"

"Yeah-yeah," Lola said. "Today school get out early."

"Das new to me. I no remembah dat."

"Gilbert, since how long you nevah drive bus already?" Lola

chided. "Things change, you know. Things change. Things not going stay dah same fo' you. Jus' because you drive bus befo' no mean things going stay dah same as befo'. We go, Lucy. Gilbert, you take care yourself, okay?"

"Okay."

Gilbert watched for a moment his sisters waddle to the rusty blue truck, then began picking up his equipment. But a wonderful idea came to him: Why not give them what he had caught to take home and eat? He called after them. The sisters stopped and turned.

"What now, Gilbert?" Lola asked.

"Here! I geev you dese fishes I caught."

He approached them with the bucket. Curious, the sisters looked in, but their faces turned to disgust at the sight of half a dozen, suffocating eyeless mullets.

"Agh, Gilbert! Whas wrong wit' dis fish?" Lola snapped. "What happened to dah eyes?"

"Dey no mo' eyes, dis kine mullet," Gilbert explained. "I caught dem in dis hole I wen dig right down the road. Daddy wen show me how when I was small-kid time. You nevah know had all dese big limestone caves underground?"

"I knew dat," Lucy answered softly. She remembered the time when as a child playing on the roadside the ground under her had caved in, the hole taking her up to the armpits; luckily, her cries of help were heard by her father. She shuddered, thinking that slimy blind mullets could have been nibbling at her toes.

"Why you like geev us dis kine fish?" Lola demanded. "Ugly! Ugly! Cannot eat dis kine 'opala."

"No . . . good eat dis kine fish," Gilbert said. "Dis is mullet. No worry 'bout dem having no mo' eyes. Mo' ono, dah taste. You try 'em. Steam 'em, Chinese style."

"Hmff." With a wave of her hand, Lola led her sister to the truck.

Dejected, Gilbert regarded the fish, nudging the bucket, then watched his sisters climb into the pickup. Lola started the truck and rolled down her window.

"See you in town tomorrow, Gilbert," she said, "at nine

o'clock sharp."

Gilbert nodded his head and waved goodbye and watched the truck make its way down the driveway, though not understanding what his sister had said.

FIVE

Two mornings later, Gilbert was awakened by a pounding on the outside wall of his bedroom. Rubbing the sleep out of his eyes, he squinted out the window and saw his sisters. He wondered why they had not come in the house; after all, he reasoned, the house was theirs, too.

"Gilbert! Gilbert!" Lola shouted. "Get up already! We like talk to you! Come outside! We like talk to you!"

"Okay, okay," Gilbert muttered. He rubbed his eyes again, then dressed.

"Gilbert dis, Gilbert dat," the other Gilbert complained.

"No complain, Gilbert," scolded the first Gilbert. "Yo' sisters outside paying you one visit. No complain."

"I should say so," said another Gilbert.

In a minute he was out on the front porch. "Lola . . . Lucy, how you folks?" he said, yawning and scratching his chest. The morning sun was on his face.

"Nevah mind dat!" Lola hurled. "How come you wasn't there yesterday? We waited fo' you so long!"

"What she talking about?" asked the second Gilbert.

"I dunno," answered the third. "Try ask her."

"Stop talking yo' nonsense," Lola ordered. "Answer my question: How come you wasn't deah yesterday?"

"Yeah, we waited so long time," Lucy added.

"What dis you talking about?" Gilbert asked.

"No act wise, Gilbert! I know you knew about it," Lola said. "You read dah letter, eh? Dah one from dah attorney?"

"What letter?"

"What letter!" Lola sighed. "No can talk sense wit' you or what? You know what letter. Dah one wen come to you special delivery. Charlie nevah wen read 'em to you? Dat Charlie!"

"Oh! Dat letter. No, I nevah read 'em. I no can read. You know dat. But Charlie read 'em to me."

"Das what I said, Gilbert!"

"But I nevah know what was about."

"Auwe, Gilbert!" Lola cried. "Waste time talkin' wit' you."

"Why dey angry at me fo'?" the third Gilbert asked.

"I dunno," answered the second. "Dah hell I know!"

"Whachu talkin' about, Gilbert?" Lucy queried.

"There he go again, talkin' to himself," Lola complained.

"But dey yo' sistahs," Gilbert added.

"I no care," the second Gilbert retorted. "Sistahs or no sistahs, dey no have to talk to me like dat. And what dey talking about anyway? I dunno what dey talking about."

"Gilbert," scolded Lucy, "make sense!"

The second Gilbert delivered a mean and hard look at the sisters.

"Gilbert," Lola said, shaking a forefinger in front of his face, "if you was one little boy, I would give you one dirty lickin' right now, talking back to yo' older sistahs. You heard?"

"No be so rude," the second Gilbert warned. "And you—make sense!"

"Eh, you no talk back to—"

The second Gilbert grabbed Lola's hand.

"Gilbert! You let my hand go right now!"

Confused, Gilbert let go. "I—sorry—"

"You sorry nothin'! How dare you touch me like dat?" Lola stepped back, grabbing hold of the porch railing to prevent herself from falling on Lucy.

"Gilbert—how can you hit yo' sistah like dat?" Lucy cried.

"But—I nevah—!"

"But you did!" Lola shot back. "You hit me! You no good brat of one brothah!"

Lola and Lucy backed down the front steps, their eyes wide with fear. Never had their kid brother talked back to them, never before had he struck any of them.

"Lola, les go!" Lucy whispered nervously. "Quick! Before he

do something else."

Lola nodded her head. She was trembling. "Gilbert . . . you going hear about dis, Gilbert. You going hear about what you jus' did to me. I swear to God, Gilbert, you going . . ."

Lucy led Lola back to the truck. They got in quickly and drove off.

Gilbert entered the house and plopped into his father's stuffed chair, disturbing years of dust. What had just happened just didn't make any sense. He brooded injuriously on the episode, until the sunlit dust particles just about settled in the room. That was when an adage of his mother by chance pressed on his conscience: When you need kokua, go ask anybody in the family fo' help. Das what the family is fo.'

Gilbert thought and thought. The only family he had in Waipuna was his two sisters. His Uncle Jacob and his wife had died a few years back, and both their son and daughter were living in Town. The rest of his mother's side of the family had moved to remote parts of the island, while his father's side resided on the outer islands. He thought more and decided to do the next best thing.

He dressed in his best clothes. Taking a half-filled bottle of Johnny Walker's Red from a kitchen shelf, he went outside and picked bunches of white ginger and ti leaves, which grew wild around the house. Then he ambled up the trail to the family cemetery.

From the trail, the cemetery was framed with kiawe trees, and the towering, deeply creviced mountain range provided an uplifting backdrop. Drifting clouds gave the mountains the sense of motion, which made Gilbert dizzy. So he sat down between the graves of his mother and father, who were buried among the ancestors of his mother's side of the family. He laid the fragrant flowers on his mother's grave, poured a generous shot of whiskey on the grave of his father, then divided the ti leaves evenly between them. He sighed. Then Gilbert the drinker asked Gilbert the non-drinker if he wanted a sip, and he was refused adamantly. Gilbert the drinker shrugged his shoulders and took a long swig from the bottle, for he thought it was rude to have their father drink alone.

"Mama . . . Papa," he began sadly, "I need help. Like you say,

Mama, when you need help you go to dah family. But Mama, I no mo' family. My sisters, dey no like me. I dunno why. Ev'rytime dey scolding-scolding me. I no think I did anything wrong. I try share my fish wit' dem. I try make dem feel at home. I dunno what fo' do. And den Charlie come and talk stink 'bout Lola and Lucy. I like punch Charlie's mouth, but no can. Charlie my good friend. And then the other time dose fancy shirt-n-tie men come visit us and they talking funny kine, 'bout money and land. I dunno what is going on, Mama . . . Papa. I dunno where I standing wit' all dis things happening. I dunno where I suppose to go fo' help."

He poured his father another shot, then drank one, too. And he waited for an answer. He watched two mynah birds yak on a branch of a kiawe tree above him. And he poured his father another shot and one for himself. And he watched the shadowy faces on the mountain range change as the sun moved over the cemetery and then over the range, disappearing. And he drank more and poured more for his father. And he slowly sank into a nostalgia, thinking about the things that were before, like Mama's pickled mangoes and stewed pigs' feet and custard pies, which he missed very, very much.

He lay down for what he supposed to be a minute, father and son having drunk the entire bottle, and he didn't wake up until much later when the mynahs above him took their morning shit, one glob landing smack on his cheek, barely missing the opening of a snoring mouth.

SIX

At the Royal Kalakaua Hotel, Neuhauser was waiting impatiently in the lobby for Wilkins. Earlier that morning, they had endured another no-compromising meeting with their Japanese national partners concerning the proposed Waipuna development. How the hell were they going to begin the project if the Japs weren't going to give them the capital they needed? After all, Hawaiian International had already invested double what the Japanese had, if one considered time and inflation. But where the hell was Hank? He had gone to his room to make a short call to the downtown office, but that was over a half hour ago. They were going to be late for that meeting in Waipuna with the Sanchez sisters. Neuhauser glanced anxiously at his watch. It would take roughly an hour to get to Waipuna. Where the hell was Hank? In bed with that baked tourist slut he picked up at the bar last night?

He saw Wilkins get out of the elevator. He stood up and made sure Wilkins saw the disgruntled expression on his face.

"Sorry, Jerre," Wilkins said.

"What the fuck were you doing? Screwing the phone?"

Wilkins grinned. "No. Don't get so jealous now, Jerre, just because I ran it back ninty-nine yards to paydirt and you got minus nineteen." He winked.

"Get off it. Let's go."

They got into the limousine that had been waiting for most of the morning. They were silent while the driver drove out of the hotel driveway and into the traffic. Then Wilkins made a comment on the futility of the morning meeting.

"Yeah, those Japs are something else," Neuhauser said caustically.

"Cool it," Wilkins whispered, nodding in the direction of the chauffeur.

"I don't give a damn if anyone hears. Christ, between dealing with them gooks and those damn fat sisters, I don't really give a shit what any of them think."

"Jerre, my boy, nowadays you can't just go straight into the jungle with a machete and compass."

Lola was out in the front yard giving her nine-year-old son lessons in catching chickens. "Sammy! Chase 'em into dah pen! Dodohead! Catch dah big one!"

Reluctantly, Sammy singled out the biggest bird from the fluttering pack. He didn't want to catch any of them, for he had gotten fond of the birds; they were his pets, and he had given each a Hawaiian name. He wasn't ready to see any of their heads chopped off, blood spurting like water spouting from a blowhole, later finding them on the dinner table fried, roasted or adobo'd.

"Sammy! Whassamattah you? You get glue on yo' feet o' what?"

Sammy stopped and pointed down the muddy driveway that was hedged with thick clusters of ti plants. A black limousine was coming up.

Quickly, Lola climbed the wooden stairs to the front door, each step wheezing with her weight, and entered the house. She glanced around the living room. Yes, things were in place, and the picture of her husband who had died in Vietnam was placed inconspicuously with the lineup of graduation pictures on top of the old console piano. She hurried into the bathroom and made sure that her makeup wasn't smeared, that every strand of hair was in place, and that the flowers tucked in her hair were just right. She regarded her profile, adjusted the straps and cups of her large brassiere, and smoothed the wrinkles of her mu'umu'u over her hips. Then, smiling and winking a naughty eye at herself, she went out to greet the haole businessmen.

The chauffeur had driven into the front yard with the intention of turning the car around, but the back tires had found a muddy spot and were spinning in place, spattering mud behind.

Lola brought her hands together in exaggerated concern. "Oh my!" she said; then, irately, "Sammy! Why you nevah tell dah driver no go in dah yard? You know get all kine wet spots!"

Finally, the driver gave up at the urging of his passengers. He got out and opened the door for the men. The haole businessmen stepped out carefully.

Lola touched the side of her hairdo and beamed a smile. "Aloha, Mr. Wilkins and Mr. Newhouse. Welcome to my humble house. Sammy, don't just stand there! Go help them!"

Wilkins smiled. "Hello, Mrs. Makanihi. Sorry we took so long to get here. We were held back a while. Seems as though we had a little car trouble."

The driver shut the door with a snap, countering Wilkins's remark with a wry grin, then went back into the car.

"Oh, that's all right, Mr. Wilkins. We live casually in Waipuna. Hawaiian-style, you know."

"I don't see your sister," Wilkins commented. "Is she coming?"

"Oh, Lucy! She always late. But she said she coming. I

talked to her on the phone this morning. Come inside. And please! Call me Lola."

Lola led the two men into her house. "Mind your shoes, please," she said to the men, who took off their shoes at the door. She offered them seats at the kitchen table.

"You have a very nice, quaint little house here, Lola," Wilkins said. "And please call me Hank."

"Hank, would you and—and—"

"Jerre," Neuhauser added dryly.

". . . would you and Jerre like a cup of coffee?"

"Sure, if it's no trouble," Wilkins said, as Neuhauser nodded in agreement.

"No problem. I have it made already."

Lola poured out three cups of freshly brewed coffee and served them.

"Milk and sugar?"

"I take mine black," Wilkins said.

"Mine, too," Neuhauser added.

"You sure you folks don't want a little bit of honey and cream?" Lola suggested.

"No, thank you."

"Didn't you say your sister was coming, too?" Neuhauser asked.

"Ah, my sister! She take ages to do anything."

"Well, I think we could start without her," Wilkins said. "You could fill her in later, couldn't you?"

Lola nodded her head.

"Well then, Jerre and I just met with Mr. Nagazaki, Mr. Iida, and Mr. Takemoto of the Tokyo Imperial Bank this morning, and we've come to a general consensus on key points for the go-ahead on the Waipuna Plan. Mrs. Makanihi—I mean, Lola—you and your sister and your respective families can be in on the making of a lot of money with that piece of land owned by your family."

"You mean my brother Gilbert's land."

"Well, yes. And that, perhaps, is where the problem lies. We've talked to your brother, and, well, frankly speaking—"

"He's lolo."

"Excuse me?"

"He's lolo. He's crazy."

"Well, I guess that's one way you can put it."

"Oh, he's lolo. And everybody knows that."

"Well, did you and your sister take our advice to see that attorney in town?"

"Yes. But my brother Gilbert, he forgot to come."

"You could still go to court and have the court appoint you power-of-attorney, with your brother in the condition he's in."

"What do you mean?"

Neuhauser sipped the coffee and made a sour face as if he had tasted mud. He hid the expression quickly.

"What I mean," Wilkins continued, "is that you and your sister can contest your brother's sole claim on that property. There's a strong precedence for such cases brought to court."

"In other words, Mrs. Makanihi," Neuhauser added, "your sister and yourself, if things work out for you, could become the legal joint owners of the property due to your brother's mental condition. At worst, you could become trustees for your brother's estate. In this situation, you still would be given control of managing his property, with the understanding that it be done in behalf of his interest."

"Is your brother married? Divorced? Does he have any children?" Wilkins asked.

"No, he's been a bachelor all his life."

"That lessens the complication. In the event of his death, then, ownership goes uncontested to you and your sister. It's a simple matter of having him sign his John Hancock at the bottom of a few documents, and that will be that."

Wilkins nodded his head in agreement.

"You mean all he gotta do is sign his name on a piece of paper and that is that?"

"Well, on several documents. But yes," Neuhauser said.

"So it's your responsibility to pursue this matter. You must reassure him that it will be in the best interest for him and the rest of the family. Your property is valuable, but only valuable if it's put to the best use."

"You mean just by him signing the documents is going to make the land belong to us?"

The men nodded their heads.

"Our advice to you and your sister," Wilkins said, "is that you see the lawyer whom we recommended and talk to him about this matter. He should help you and answer any questions that you might have. In fact, if it's all right with you, we'll go ahead and schedule an appointment for you and your sister. We'll also inform him about what we've just talked about. To save time, of course."

"Oh, would you!" Lola was pleased. "You two are so nice, coming here and giving me all this good advice. You would do that for me and my sister?"

Wilkins nodded his head again, half closing his eyes to show her the extent of his sincerity. "We surely will."

They got up to leave while graciously refusing Lola's offer of more coffee.

The driver had somehow managed to get the limousine out of the mud spot. The businessmen and Lola exchanged goodbyes and then they were off. Lola waved goodbye with a broad smile until the limousine disappeared around a turn of ti plants.

"Mama, what dah haole men wen say?" Sammy asked.

"Nevah mind what dah haoles wen say! Das not yo' business. You caught dah chicken yet?"

The limousine passed through the small village of Waipuna and, after crossing a narrow bridge that spanned a stream which fed several taro paddies, sped down the two-lane highway towards Town.

"Well, that wasn't bad, was it?" Wilkins said, slapping Neuhauser on the thigh.

"No. I've been in worse meetings. But the coffee! Did you taste the coffee? It tasted like mud!"

"Did you even see me touch the mug?"

Neuhauser grinned. "Hey, that Lola gal has got an eye for you."

"Oh yeah?"

They laughed.

The men watched the greenery pass by for a while.

"We better get hold of James Fogarty," Wilkins said finally, "and get him to draft those documents right away."

"You think Lola and her sister are going to go down soon?"

"Tomorrow morning."

"Tomorrow morning? How's that?"

Wilkins turned to Neuhauser with a knowing smile. "We'll bowl them over with kindness. I'll call her up tonight, make some small talk, then I'll tell her I've made arrangements for the limousine to pick her and her sister up at nine sharp tomorrow morning. At her house. That'll knock her flat on her back."

"Boy, Hank, you have a way with these local women, don't you?"

Wilkins smiled at his partner, winking an eye.

One minute after lecturing Sammy on his ineptness at chicken catching, Lola was on the phone to Lucy. The phone rang a dozen times before Lucy answered, panting like a dog under a hot sun.

"Lucy! How come you no answer dah phone?"

Lucy was going to say "What you t'ink I doing right now?" but Lola didn't give her time to catch her breath and told her that the two haoles from the development company had come over with a suggestion that she and Lucy would be foolish not to take. Lucy asked her what kind of advice it was, and Lola told her a confusing version of what "the power-of-attorney" meant. Before she could give Lucy time to digest her explanation, Lola asked her if she thought the tall haole was good-looking or not.

Lola waited for a long moment, almost ready to hang up and redial Lucy's number, when finally Lucy aspirated loudly. "I dunno, Lola. But you know what?"

"What?"

"I t'ink Gilbert getting wise to what we doing."

"Whachu mean?"

"Gilbert came ovah heah dis morning, and he brought wit' him dah letter dah attorney guy wen send to him."

"Whachu mean by dat? So what you wen do? What he wen do?"

"Nothing."

"Whachu mean you nevah do nothing? *He* nevah do nothing?"

Sammy opened the kitchen door, cradling Laka the chicken in his arms. His eyes were moist. "Mama . . . dah chicken."

Covering the mouthpiece with her hand, she glared at Sammy. "You cannot see Mommy on dah phone wit' Auntie Lucy?! Go away! No bother me right now!"

Sammy backed out of the kitchen, closing the door behind him. He stroked his chicken lovingly. Then, with a glimmer in his eyes, he wiped away his tears and shrugged his shoulders, setting the chicken on the porch and shooing it off. "Run away! Hide, baby!" he commanded, and the chicken flapped its wings and fled into a ti bush.

In the house, Lola asked Lucy, "Whas dat again now? You said Gilbert know what going on?"

"I think so. He had dis funny kine look on his face. He was smiling. But I could read his eyes. Jus' like he was laughing to himself. If you ask me, his eyes looked kinda spooky."

"Dat Gilbert. He really going into dah deep end. Our own bruddah."

"Maybe we should forget about it."

"Forget about what?"

"Dah pepahs wit' dah attorney. Das Gilbert's land, not really ours."

"Whachu talking about, Lucy? Dah land worth millions of dollars. No ways I going let our lolo bruddah get dah money and us get nothing. I not going let all dat money slip through my fingers. I not going live in dis rathole dah rest of my life."

"Den what we going do?"

There was long moment of silence. Then Lucy asked Lola if she was still there on the phone, to which Lola responded, "Wait— wait." Then, as if an eternity had passed, Lola whispered, "Listen, Lucy, dis what we going do."

SEVEN

All Gilbert had done was bring the attorney's letter to Lucy's, hoping she would read and interpret it for him. But when he presented her the letter, she had turned pale. Gilbert responded quickly by getting her a chair, which she refused. He began to feel uncomfortable, Lucy staring at him with bewildering eyes and not saying anything at all. Finally he excused himself, thanked her out of courtesy and left the house, thinking perhaps it was the fish smell on his clothes that had made her sick.

He stopped at the general store on the way home. At the cash register, reading the afternoon paper, was Jimson Nakakura, who had taken over the family business shortly after his old man had started seeing the frogmen coming out of the mangroves. Jimson was Gilbert's classmate and fellow teammate on the cellar high school football team. In the good old days after graduation, they had often shared beers during warm afternoons, but since Gilbert had started making pupule-talk, the storekeeper had slowly distanced himself from his old buddy. When Gilbert entered the store, Jimson raised an eyebrow, then went back to reading the newspaper.

"Jimson . . . so whas new?" Gilbert asked amicably. He got himself a favorite strawberry-flavored soda from the cooler and set it on the counter.

"Nothing much," Jimson mumbled. "Twenty-five cents."

"You know my sister, you think she going lolo o' what?"

"Twenty-five cents, Gilbert."

"I dunno. But funny kine, dah way she act wit' me. I was at her house right now and she give me one funny kine look, jus' like I get leprosy. Maybe was the fish smell on me. I smell like mullet?"

"Twenty-five cents. No, I no smell one mullet."

Gilbert searched for a quarter in his pocket and set it on the worn rubber counter mat, between the "n" and "k" of "Thank You."

"Thirty cents, if you going take dah bottle," Jimson added.

Gilbert searched again, gave Jimson the extra nickel, then said goodbye, leaving the store a bit confused at the cold treatment his friend had given him, something he had been noticing for a while but just couldn't get himself to ask his friend why. Why Jimson had all of a sudden turned unfriendly was an enigma to Gilbert, for they had been buddies ever since he could remember: they had spent a childhood together swimming in Waipuna Stream and fishing for blind mullet in the sacred underground limestone caves; they were co-captains on the football team; and, while in high school, Gilbert had dated Jimson's cousin and Jimson had dated Gilbert's cousin, whom Jimson later married. Gilbert just couldn't figure it out.

And while walking down the road, he was passed by several cars, and he wondered why none of them stopped to offer him a ride; they had always before. Everyone knew everyone else in Waipuna, and offering someone a ride was a custom of Waipuna life. He finished the soda, tossing the bottle into the bush, then thought that perhaps it was the fishy smell that was turning people off to him. Jimson was probably being nice when he said that he didn't smell anything fishy. With that problem resolved, he smiled and whistled all the way home.

At home, he found a jar of pickled mangoes on the porch. He studied it in the light of the waning sun, marvelling at its rich red color. It looked delicious. He wondered who would have left him such a delicacy. He sat on the top step, drawing in a tired breath. It had been a long walk back home. Not one person had stopped to give him a lift, but that was okay since he would have refused the offer anyway, not wanting to get into someone's car and stink it up. He looked at the pickled mangoes again and decided to eat one. Opening the wide-mouth jar, he took in the rich, vinegary aroma, which reminded him of the way Mama's pickled mangoes smelled. Had Mama come by and left him this treat? Only Mama could have made something that smelled as delicious as this. No one in Waipuna knew how to make pickled mangoes the way she did.

He fished out a large slice, took in the entire piece without a bite, sucked the sour juices, then crunched it up, his tongue shrivelling in delight. And he kept on eating until all that was left was the liquid. Which he drank down, too.

Only Mama could make pickled mangoes like this. Gilbert looked towards the back of the house, in the direction of the family cemetery. Perhaps Mama had heard him.

"Mama, did you make dis?"

"Don't be silly. Mama's in heaven. How she going come back down here and make you pickled mango?"

"No, must be Mama. Try taste. Only her can make something ono like dis."

"I no like dat. Too sour. How you can stand dat?"

"Ono. You missing out. No . . . only Mama can make something like dis. Only Mama."

"You right! Mama did it. I saw her."

"You nevah! You was wit' Gilbert all dis time."

"No, I believe him. I really think Mama dah one wen make 'em. Only her can."

"You two folks full of shit. Wise up. You guys lolo or what? Maybe you was dah one who wen make dis and wen make 'em fo' fool me!"

EIGHT

It was strange. Every other afternoon for a week Gilbert would find on the front porch one of his favorite foods that his mother used to prepare. First, it was that jar of pickled mangoes. Two days later was Mama's teriyaki dried akule. Next was a freshly baked custard pie. And now, today, roast chicken basted with Mama's own coconut barbeque sauce. What was next? Her specialty . . . stewed pigs' feet with guava?

Or was one of his sisters behind all of this? That was a consideration. But he thought about it for a short while and disregarded the idea. First, his sisters had enough sense not to leave food outside on the porch where it would be fair game for the wild dogs; they would have left it in the house. Second, his sisters had never invited him over for dinner, so why would they cook for him now? And finally—the most convincing reason why they could not be the responsible party—both of his sisters were lousy cooks. There was no way in hell that either of his sisters could cook like Mama. This, he knew, as a fact.

It had to be Mama cooking all of these goodies, Gilbert concluded. Sitting on the top of the porch steps, Gilbert looked at the drifting clouds and smiled. Then he prayed and crossed himself. He was happy. Mama was looking down on him and giving him a supporting hand. He was not alone anymore. What Mama had told him about the importance of the family was definitely true. He was truly happy.

With that profound realization, he hurried into the house, took another half-spent bottle of Johnny Walker's and went out to the back.

"Where you going wit' dat bottle? Drink again?"

In the back of the house, he cut an armful of wild ginger and heliconia. With the bottle of whiskey and flowers, Gilbert lumbered up the trail to the family cemetery, humming a tune, then singing it aloud. It was a song that he forgot the title to, a song that Trish Kobashigawa and he had danced to in the eighth grade, their first dance.

"Oh . . . so you remember dat song? Was dah ninth-grade school dance, yeah?"

"No. Eighth grade."

"Okay-okay. Dah eighth grade. Dah time you and Trish Kobashigawa—"

"Who dat?"

Wheezing when he got to the top of the trail, Gilbert plopped between his parents' graves and caught his breath. Then he arranged the flowers fan-like over his mother's grave and thanked her. He poured a shot on the ground over his father and asked Gilbert the drinker if he wanted a drink, which, of course, was not refused. Then he turned to Mama, hinted for a platter of either stewed pigs' feet with guava or pulehu short ribs—whichever was easier to make—thanked her and returned to the house.

NINE

Lola visited Gilbert early one morning, calling him through the dusty kitchen screen. Her voice was as sweet as guava nectar.

Gilbert came to the door, rubbing his eyes. "Lola . . . what you doing heah?" He yawned, then smiled peacefully. "Long time no see."

"Gilbert, I can come in?"

"Sure, no need ask. Dis yo' house, too."

Lola rolled her shoulders and grinned. "I guess so."

Inside, she seated herself at the kitchen table. "Gilbert, you keeping dis house real nice. You can make me one cup coffee?"

Without a word, Gilbert set a small pot of water on the gas stove.

"When was the last time you painted the kitchen? Look so nice, the color."

Gilbert scanned the kitchen walls. "I dunno. Look the same to me, j'like the last time I wen look at 'em."

Lola gave the room another look-over and shrugged her shoulders. "Tell me, Gilbert. What you do over here all by yo'self? You watch TV all day long?"

"Sometimes I watch TV. But most times I go fishing fo' dah kine . . ." He stopped himself. He remembered the trauma he had created the time he offered Lola and Lucy the blind mullet to take home. "Oh, I catch anykine. Crabs. Anykine fish."

Lola closed her eyes, trying not to think about the translucent blind mullet. But the picture came to her mind anyway. Her stomach became queasy.

"Gilbert . . . Gilbert, so how you been?"

"Hah? Oh, you asked me dat already."

"I mean what else you do here?"

"Oh, I jus' remember something I gotta tell you, something real good." He poured the hot water into two cups, then stirred a teaspoon of instant coffee in each. He gave one to Lola and sat down next to her with his.

"I like cream and sugar wit' mine," Lola said.

Gilbert brought her what she needed.

"And so, what you was tryin' tell me now, about something good?"

"Yeah," he said, smiling. "You know, Mama been cooking fo' me. She been making me all my favorite kine foods. I not kiddin' you."

Lola smiled to herself. "Oh, yeah? What you mean? You

mean Mama been cookin' fo' you? How can?"

"I know hard to believe, Lola, but fo' real. I been getting all dese foods."

"All dese foods?" She tittered. The pickled mangoes that she made was so sour, she wouldn't dare give it to anyone. Except maybe Gilbert. Everything tasted good to him. "So you think Mama wen make you the pickled mango?"

"How you know was pickled mango?"

"Oh—uh—"

"She gave you too?"

"Yeah—no—I mean, yeah."

"She gave you her custard pie too?"

"Custard pie?"

"Yeah. And she gave you her coconut chicken?"

"Gilbert. You going a little bit too far. Was only pickled mango."

"Oh, I guess she nevah have nuff ingredients," he said, his voice and eyes dropping. He became sorry that he blurted out what he did. Mama probably didn't give Lola what she gave him, and maybe by saying so he had hurt Lola's feelings. "Oh, but dah mango was good, yeah?" he added quickly.

"Yeah . . . was good."

But Lola saw opportunity in her brother's smile. It not going take much to make him look bad, she thought. Just one bottle of pickled mango and look at him get all carried away.

"And den, what brings you home?" Gilbert asked.

"Gilbert. I like ask you something dat I like you t'ink real hard about."

"Shoot. Ask."

"Gilbert, what you t'ink if Lucy and me, if we both start taking care of you and also dis place?"

Gilbert's eyes crossed. He shook his head to get rid of Lola's double image. "What you said?" he asked.

"I said we can take care of you. If you like."

"Oh, das nice of you. But I okay."

"Oh. I heard some strange things happening over here. Das

why I thought I come here and ask you if you need help."

"Strange things?"

"Yeah. Strange things."

"Like what?"

"Somebody said dat you told him dat you saw Mama's ghost floating around, bringing you things fo' eat. Of course, you know I believe in dah spirits, like dat. But you know, as well as I know,"—clearing her throat—"that ghost no can cook."

"But I telling you fo' one fact. It *is* Mama cooking all dat food. Honest. Fo' real."

"But fo' real," Gilbert the drinker said, finally aroused from his sleepwalk. He yawned. "Lucy, why you talking like that about Mama?"

"Gilbert. Wake up. Dis is Lola. I said you imagining you seeing Mama's ghost floating around."

"Imagining what?" Gilbert the drinker said. "Dat Mama's ghost is floating around? You no can see her right now?"

"Gilbert! Try make sense!" She scanned the ceiling with a wary eye, then gave Gilbert a hard look. Gilbert the drinker began laughing. "What you pulling over me, Gilbert? Make sense, all right?"

But Gilbert could not remember telling anyone about Mama's ghost since he had never witnessed it. Gilbert the drinker had probably made up a story and told everyone about it. Damn drunk. Or perhaps the delivery boy had made it up. But Mama's food was for real.

"Mama is . . . she's not here anymore," Lola said. "Gilbert, I t'ink you imagining all dis. Somebody tol' me dat you said dat you saw Mama's ghost floating around. Maybe living heah all by yo'self is not too good."

"Somebody saw Mama's ghost?"

"I feel like I talking in circles! Gilbert—you listening to me or what?"

"But you said somebody saw Mama's ghost?"

"Yeah. Somebody tol' me about it."

"Who was it?"

"Oh, Gilbert, I don't remember. But I t'ink you been living heah too long by yo'self. Let me ask you again. You like yo' two big sistahs take care you o' what?"

Gilbert the drinker yawned.

"Ah . . . I dunno."

"We can take care you good. Feed you. Clothe you. You no haf' to worry 'bout anything."

"Ah, I guess sounds all right."

"Sounds all right?" Gilbert the drinker interjected. "You like I live wit' you and Lola?! You gotta be crazy!"

"Shut up!" said an irate Gilbert. "No listen to him, Lucy."

Stunned, Lola stared at Gilbert.

"No listen to him, Lucy. He crazy."

"Gilbert, Lucy and me—*Lola*—offering you one situation of a lifetime. And what I hear you telling me?"

"No listen to him, Lucy."

"*Lola!*"

"I sorry, Lola." To Gilbert the drinker: "You bettah shut yo' mouth o' I going hide dah booze, you unnerstand?"

There was no rebuttal from Gilbert the drinker.

"Listen, Lola. Let me think about it, Lola. You know, I kinda set in my own ways already."

"Gilbert, I no have time to wait. You gotta make up yo' mind right now. I nevah come all dah way heah fo' nothin'. I mean, my time is valuable but I came out heah to try help you out."

"Oh, I guess sounds okay wit' me."

"It's a good idea, Gilbert. You no haf' to worry 'bout nothin'."

"Is a terrible idea!"

"What!"

"No listen to him," Gilbert said apologetically. "He had little bit too much last night. But I guess it is one good idea to me. What I haf' to do?"

"Oh, nothing much! All you gotta do is come sign some pepahs at the attorney's office in Town."

"Where dat?"

"Town! Downtown, silly! But you knew dat, right, Gilbert?"

He nodded. He was confused like hell. "But I no can read, Lola."

"Oh, no worry. I can explain everything you gotta know at the attorney's office. The attorney can explain everything, too. No worry. We family, Gilbert, right?" She waited for Gilbert's answer. "Well?"

"Yeah, I guess so."

"All right, den. Everything going be all right. You watch. Tomorrow I going swing by here and pick you up. Den we go to the attorney's office. Okay?"

"Okay."

"Okay, den. Tomorrow is the seventeenth. I pick you up at eight o' clock sharp." She picked up her bag and started towards the door.

Gilbert the drinker remembered that the next day was exactly one year that Tricia Kobashigawa had left him. "Yeah-yeah," he grumbled.

"Huh?" Lola turned.

"Oh, nothing," said Gilbert, trying to cover for his double.

"Oh, and by dah way, Gilbert. What kine coffee you buy? Dah cheap kine? Ho! Taste like mud."

"Oh, but why you bring her up now?"

"Hah? What you talking about, Gilbert?"

"Nothing! Nothing! Jus' t'inking aloud."

"Cause I no care fo' dat damn bitch, running off wit' dah fuckin' haole."

Lola looked at her brother with caution, then slipped out of the house.

"Dat damn bitch. I kill dem both, her and dat fuckin' haole."

TEN

Later that morning, Lola and Lucy drove to town for a meeting with the attorney who went over the necessary forms that they would need to have Gilbert sign. Then the sisters left the office and walked down the main street for about a block with Lola doing all the small talk about how fair the settlement would be, how Gilbert really didn't deserve the property, and why they should be the rightful heirs since they had taken care of Mama and Papa during the time when it really counted (when Gilbert was in the service). Lucy stopped her sister's monologue.

"I no trust dat haole."

"Who you talking about? What haole?" asked a puzzled Lola.

"Dat haole. Dah attorney."

"What you mean you no trust him. He's one attorney. He know his business. If you trust one priest, you can trust one attorney-of-law."

"So you really t'ink dis thing we going sign is all right, den? Smell kinda funny to me, if you ask me."

"Eh . . . no worry. Dis attorney guy, he akamai, he's all right. He knows his business. The legal profession is his business."

"I no trust him. Dah way he look. Dah smile. Fake. And den his secretary. Local, but kinda unfriendly dah way she talk."

"Ho! Hard talk to you. I said dah attorney is all right. You no can trust my judgement? And dah secretary, why bring her up? She secondary. But dah attorney, das his job, to tell you dah bare facts of dah law. Who else you goin' trust?"

"I can trust you. But I no trust dat haole."

"Den who you goin' trust?"

"If was one Hawaiian lawyer, maybe I get mo' trust in him."

"Hawaiian. Haole. Japanee. All dah same, Lucy. Dah main thing he can talk good. And dis attorney he smart fo' talk."

"Too smart, you ask me. He talk too smooth, everything sounds all right. Das what I no trust. He's one smooth talker. I no like smooth talkers."

"Nevah mind. Everything going be all right. Legally speaking, the property is going be ours. Lucy, we going make plenny money. We going be rich . . . millionaires! Dat no make you feel good?"

Lucy thought about what the money could bring. Maybe they could dump her husband's old truck and get him a well-deserved new one. Maybe she'd buy Clarence a brand new four-wheel drive, the one he always so silently admired when watching the commercial on television. She knew he liked that truck. His eyes would soften at the commercial, and she almost could hear the little boy in him begging for the toy. But of course he would never say anything, her husband was the quiet type. She loved her husband and wanted to please him. All the guys he worked with had new trucks and four-wheel drives, and it was about time that he could show off, too. And she'd buy her kids new clothes that fit well, not the hand-me-downs from Lola or clothes bought on sale that were out of style. Hoku was getting to that age when wearing the right clothes meant a lot. And Lyle was always outgrowing his clothes every three or four months. And then she'd get things for herself. A new dress. A trip to the beauty salon. There were so many things to be had with money. A new couch. Maybe one of those fancy microwave ovens.

Maybe Lola was right, that the money was really theirs, that they had more of a rightful claim to the property than Gilbert, who had no purpose in life but to fish for blind mullets or sit all day in front of the television, watching the game shows.

Lucy's eyes fell to the ground, her head shaking.

"Now what!" Lola gave her younger sister a hard look. "Eh, you lucky I brought you into dis deal."

"I dunno, Lola. I mean, I feeling kinda funny now, kinda low, how we trying to take dah land from Gilbert."

"No say dat. It's our land, too."

"I know. But was actually fo' Gilbert. Das how Mama and Papa made it. Both you and me, we get houses already. Gilbert no get nothing. What he going do when we sell dah land and he no mo' place to stay? He going stay wit' you?"

"Dah hell he going stay wit' me! Dat pupule-head bruddah of mine?"

"He cannot stay wit' me, Lola. We no mo' room in my house. But you get plenny room yo' house. Only you and Sammy."

"Dah hell he going stay wit' me!"

Lola strutted ahead a few steps, stopped and turned. "Fo' Chrissakes, Lucy! What is all dis business you talking about? Why you changing yo' mind so often? One wind come and you going already. And you dah one who was so strong fo' us fo' get our rightful share!"

"But Lola, you was dah—"

"Nevah mind! I askin' you dis. You in dis or not? Tell me, right now."

"Lola, I don't feel right about all of dis."

"Now you saying you 'don't feel right.' Come on, Lucy, you wasn't born yesterday. I know as well as you know dat all dis we doing is right. Right?"

Lucy nodded her head.

"Den whas stopping you? Evah since we got into dat attorney's office, I seen dat funny look on yo' face. Are you in or not? Tell me. You gotta tell me now." Angrily, Lola turned and stomped down the sidewalk.

Lucy called after her.

"What you like now?" Lola asked.

"I think I going back and tell dah attorney I changing my mind."

"Whoa, Lucy! Why you going do something stupid like dat?"

"No call me stupid, Lola. I not stupid." For a moment, Lucy's eyes darkened. "I changing my mind. I no like anything to do wit' dis. I mean dah money is something else. All dah things we can buy wit' it and all dat jazz. But dah land's Gilbert's. And das dat."

"What you talking, Lucy? You like pour all dat money down the drain?"

"I been losing sleep t'inking 'bout all dis, Lola."

Lola approached her sister, sensing that the argument was being lost. "Oh c'mon, Lucy. What we doing is the right thing to do. If Mama and Papa was alive, dey would say what we doing is right."

"I think Mama and Papa would be scolding us. I tell you, Lola, I never get one good night's sleep fo' one long time, t'inking about all of dis."

Lola smiled. "Lucy, I know you get one good conscience. Das why I know Gilbert not going get left out. I t'ink about him, too. In fact, I really t'ink about him plenty. What we doing all dis fo' is really fo' our families. Right? Mama and Papa told us dat their land is our land, and dah land is fo' dah benefit fo' everybody in dah family.

Right?"

Lucy drew in a large breath of air, then let it out with some of her anger.

"So," Lola continued, "rightfully we are doing dah right thing. You see what I saying?"

"Yeah . . . I guess so."

"You know the things I said about Gilbert, I nevah really mean fo' say it dat way. Sometimes, things come out wrong. Well, maybe things come out right but dey sound wrong. But ev'rything going be all right. Look, if haf' to, I take Gilbert in my house. Promise. If make you feel bettah. All right? Make you feel bettah?"

Lucy shook her head. "No. Something still wrong. I felt 'em the minute I stepped into the lawyer's office today. Something wrong. I jus' have dat funny feeling."

"No be silly. Nothing wrong. Sometimes the feeling is right, but sometimes you gotta t'ink out the feeling if it is right or not. You know what I mean?"

Lucy rolled her shoulders.

"Come," Lola said. "We go the coffee shop down the street. I treat you lunch. C'mon. Hurry up. Before the lunch crowd beat us to it."

Lucy took in another deep breath, then nodded her head, feeling a paradoxical sense of clarity and confusion.

"No worry, Lucy, no worry," Lola consoled. "Ev'rything going be all right. We cannot jus' leave Gilbert hanging wit' no place to go, right? We family, right? We going take care. No worry. Ev'rything is going take care of itself."

ELEVEN

Gilbert was walking home on the main road after an afternoon fishing the underground limestone caves when he came across old man Nakakura by the roadside. The old man, with his nose pointing and lips protruding, was silently facing the mangroves. He was leaning on a straight branch of guava, his body stiffened at a slant as if frozen the moment after throwing out a fish net; the essential picture could be depicted by the Chinese character for "man": 人 .

Gilbert stopped, aborted a conversation with himself about the difference between blind mullets and regular mullets, and watched the old man, who seemed oblivious to his presence. A breeze came, bringing the rotten smell of the mudflats, and Nakakura-san moved but slightly.

"Gilbert," the old man whispered, without looking at him, "no bother me now. I hear dem buggahs coming."

Gilbert looked into the mangroves. "Who? Who coming?"

"Be quiet. No talk so loud. Dem buggahs. Dah frogmen."

"Hah?"

"Jus' shut up. Keep quiet. You going scare dem away. I trying catch dem by surprise."

Gilbert stopped his tongue, his eyes widening with caution.

"Deah! You heard dat?"

Gilbert thought he heard the scurry of a mongoose in the bush, but he kept his opinion to himself. Who was he to challenge the venerable wisdom of Nakakura-san?

"You heard dat?" the old man asked impatiently.

"Heard what?"

"Dah sound. Dah frogmen's sound."

"Yeah-yeah. I heard dat." He heard another scurry in the bush, but this time it didn't sound like a mongoose. "I heard dat one," he said in a whisper. "You heard dat one?"

Old man Nakakura didn't make a sound or move.

"So what you goin' do, Uncle-san?" Gilbert pressed.

The old man remained in his awkward position, now looking like a cat (to Gilbert) that was a jump away from a flock of fat pigeons. Then, after a tense minute: "Huh? What you said, Gilbert?"

Gilbert had almost forgotten what he had asked, the suspense and chill of the moment (though the warm afternoon sun was bathing them both) almost vanquishing the idea of the question. He took in a shallow breath and resuscitated the idea to new life: "What you goin' do, Uncle-san?"

The old man narrowed his eyes and gave him a disquieting look, as if Gilbert had asked a very stupid question. "What I goin' do? What I goin' do!"

Gilbert's eyes winced in embarrassment.

"I goin' knock dem buggahs' heads, das what I goin' do," he raged. He pointed his stick at the mangroves. "Dem buggahs like come in heah and make trouble. Dey like take ovah. Dem buggahs, dey no believe in nothin'. Dey no respect nothin'. All dey like is make trouble fo' ev'rybody else but not fo' demselfs. I goin' smash dem ugly heads in." He took a level swing at the air with the guava stick. "I goin' bash dey heads in, make dem regret dey even wen think 'bout coming heah making trouble." He coughed harshly. "I goin' . . . I goin' save Waipuna from dese fuckin', sonavabitch frogmen."

Then he turned to Gilbert and gave him a hard look that made him shiver. "And you . . . you goin' help me? Or you goin' be one 'nother chickenshit, j'like all dah res'?"

It wasn't a question that Gilbert heard but an ultimatum. Without thinking, Gilbert nodded his head.

"Good." A smile blossomed from Nakakura's hardened face, though short-lived. "Deah . . . you see dat ovah deah?" he said, pointing to an object in the wild grass about ten yards away. "Pick up dat thing ovah deah right now and come back right away."

Gilbert dropped his fishing gear and set the bucket of suffocating blind mullet on the ground. He looked for what Nakakura-san was pointing at. "Whas dat, Uncle-san? Whas dat ovah deah you pointing at?"

"Dah stick. Go get dah stick."

"I no see one stick."

The old man grunted. "You gotta go deah and get it in order fo' you to see it, Gilbert. Use yo' common sense."

Gilbert tramped into the tall grass, found the stick and hurried back with it to the old man.

"Good." The old man nodded with satisfaction, but another sound in the mangroves wiped away a surfacing smile. "Deah! You heard dat? Dey getting ready!"

"Ready fo' what?"

"Nevah mind. *We* gotta get ready."

Before Gilbert could ask "Get ready fo' do what?" the old man gripped the guava stick hard, his wiry arms now looking like the bumpy convolutions of a bittermelon. He raised the stick high above his head and growled.

Watching Nakakura-san, Gilbert followed suit, though not holding his stick as high as the old man. He peered into the shadowy mangroves, his mouth suddenly feeling dry. A shiver passed through him.

Nakakura-san's growl grew steadily until it culminated in a fiery loud "Banzai!" whereupon the old man hobbled fearlessly into the wild grass towards the mangroves, waving the stick above his head like an old samurai rushing towards a clash of swords. Not wanting to be left behind, Gilbert followed, brandishing his weapon and uttering a cry that perhaps his ancestors used when charging into battle: "Aaagggghhh!!!"

They yelled their battle cries while slashing the defenseless leaves and branches of the mangroves. Suddenly there was a huge burst of fluttering, as if the mangroves had come alive. The men stopped their attack on the helpless mangroves, their eyes darting, searching for the source of the sound. The fluttering pulsed, lifted from the trees and dissipated in the direction of the ocean. Then there was silence.

The old man staggered out of the bush and signaled for Gilbert to follow him. Back on the road, Nakakura-san pointed at a diminishing cloud of seabirds.

"Birds," Gilbert gasped.

"Dah frogmen," the old man corrected.

Gilbert looked at the birds again. "Dah frogmen," he said between wheezes.

With a smile as bright as the morning, Nakakura-san held a firm hand out to Gilbert. "Congratulations, Gilbert! You and me, we jus' save Waipuna from dem bastards."

Confused, Gilbert shook the old man's vigorous hands.

"You know, Gilbert, evah since you wen quit yo' job driving dah school children to school, I used to t'ink you was one crazy man. One pupule. But now,"—swallowing, a choke in his voice—"I know I was wrong fo' t'inking you was crazy. You all right, Gilbert. You all right." He gazed at the white clouds and then at the mangroves, his eyes moistening. "You and me . . . we saved Waipuna."

Gilbert liked the moment. A moment like this had been denied him for a long, long time. The warmth from the praise and recognition gave him a feeling of celebration.

"Uncle-san, we go make party at my house!"

"You get saké?" the old man quickly returned.

"Saké? Oh, no. I no mo' saké. But I get whiskey."

The old man put an arm around Gilbert's shoulders, and they started down the road towards Gilbert's house, a mere three miles away but a long enough distance for the old man to teach Gilbert a Japanese drinking song and for them to indulge in braggadocio about their glorious victory.

When they reached the house, their voices dry and ragged from singing too many stanzas without a drink, Gilbert found another jar of pickled mangoes on the porch. Attached to it was a note. Gilbert sat at the top of the porch steps, unfolded the note, then gave it to Nakakura-san.

"Uncle-san, you can read dis fo' me?"

"You read it yo'self."

"I . . . I no can read, Uncle-san."

"You mean you wen go school, graduated, and nevah wen learn how read?" Gilbert's eyes drifted to the lowest step. "Ahh!" the old man aspirated. He patted Gilbert on the back. "What dah hell, Gilbert. You no need read schoolbooks fo' drive bus. Anyway, I no can read wit'out my specs. What fo' you like read dah pepah fo' anyway? Jus' eat dah mango!"

Gilbert opened the jar and offered it to the old man, who made a sour face.

"I no like dat. Make my insides all upside down. But where dah whiskey?"

Gilbert went into the house and brought out a brand new bottle.

"Gilbert," the old man said after his fourth shot, "you know I one old man already. But what I going tell you is important. Come closer and listen good."

Gilbert moved a couple of inches towards Nakakura.

"You know, today was one great day in Waipuna history. But nobody knows dat. But das all right. Dah hell wit' dem all. Dey no unnerstand."

"Yeah, Uncle-san."

"No talk!" the old man scowled. "You listen good!"

"Yeah, Uncle-san."

"I said no talk! Listen!"

Gilbert was going to say he was sorry, but this time he held his tongue.

"You know, Gilbert, how long I been telling ev'rybody dah frogmen coming. But nobody like believe me. But you saw today. Dah frogmen, dey fo' real! And dis is not dah first time dah frogmen wen come, you know. Dey come many times already. But you gotta be ready. Das why you always see me looking, watching, getting ready fo' dem try come in again and try run ovah Waipuna."

He emptied his shot glass with a tilt of his head. Gilbert poured him another, which the old man drank immediately. Nakakura wiped his mouth with the palm of his hand.

"But I stay getting old, Gilbert. No can stay keep watch ovah ev'rything, ev'ryday. So now is dah time I start t'inkin' 'bout dah future. Das why I like you listen carefully."

He extended forward the empty shot glass, which Gilbert filled promptly.

"Gilbert, I like you be dah next Watcher of Waipuna. Is one hard job, one tough job, but haf' to be done. You not working right now, eh?"

Gilbert shook his head, afraid to say anything.

The old man's head was unsteady, his eyes momentarily crossed, but he sat up straight and took in a deep breath, and that seemed to clear everything.

"Gilbert," he began, his voice deepened. "I like appoint you take my place. I like you be my next-in-line. I like you be dah new Watcher of Waipuna."

Gilbert didn't know if he should be happy or sad, if he should celebrate or whimper. Warm sweat rolling down his face quickly turned cold from a sea breeze. His mouth opened, but no words could come out.

Nakakura-san seemed pleased by his choice. He toasted Gilbert, several times, drinking the whiskey as if it were water. Gilbert missed the shot glass on one pour and splashed whiskey on a porch step.

"Gilbert! Whassamattah you? No waste! Hooo! Whas wrong wit' you? You nervous or what?"

Nakakura-san grabbed the bottle by the neck and poured the whiskey himself. As if he were a connoisseur, he eyeballed the shot of whiskey at arm's length, then sipped it. Then he regarded the tension on Gilbert's face.

"Gilbert? Whassamattah you? Calm down. Dis is one big honor. To be dah Watcher of Waipuna." He belched. "C'mon. What you got to say fo' yo'self?"

Relieved that he was finally allowed to speak, he opened his mouth to express his confusion. But again, nothing came out.

"So Gilbert, dis means"—another sip—"dat you gotta patrol wit' me so you can learn dah ropes on how to be one Watcher. But anyway, congratulations."

The old man toasted Gilbert again. Gilbert clinked the old man's shot glass with the near-empty bottle, though he did not drink.

"So what dis means, Uncle-san," Gilbert finally blurted out. "What dis means, being dah—dah—dah—Watcher of Waipuna?"

"Yeah-yeah. I tell you."

The last drops of the whiskey went into Nakakura-san's glass. The old man set the glass down on the step. He straightened his back, twisted it right to left to right to . . . until several vertebrae cracked dully. Then he worked on his neck until it, too, cracked to his satisfaction.

"Dis means, Gilbert," the old man said finally, "dat you responsible fo' dah safety and welfare of Waipuna whenevah dah frogmen attack."

Gilbert was going to ask "But who really is dah frogmen?" but stopped himself; Nakakura-san might get angry at him for asking another stupid question. Instead, he asked, "So what else this job means?"

The old man nodded his head and said, "Dis, I tell you . . ." He drank the last shot in a slurpy gulp, handing the empty shot glass to Gilbert. With his reddened eyes focusing and unfocusing on Gilbert, he muttered, "Tomorrow." Then he rose and reeled down the steps and onto the driveway. Halfway down the driveway, Nakakura turned and shouted to Gilbert, "We start tomorrow. Tomorrow morning. Meet me by dah old pig slaughter house."

TWELVE

"Dat damn Gilbert! Dat damn stupidhead bruddah of mine!"

Sammy, sitting at the table in his Auntie Lucy's kitchen, peeped up at his mother's raving, glanced at his auntie sitting next to him, then returned to his beef stew and rice dinner. Secretly, he thought that Auntie Lucy's stew was the best in Waipuna, better than his Mom's.

"Lola, you gotta calm down," advised Lucy. "You can get ulcers."

"How can I calm down when we get such one lolo fo' one bruddah?"

"But he's our bruddah."

Lucy regarded the weather through her kitchen window. It had been overcast the entire day, but not one drop of rain had fallen.

"I no care if he's our bruddah. You no see, Lucy? You can geev him all kine gifts li' dat, but dat lolohead not going be thankful. I betchu he nevah even read dah note we left him. Ho! I felt like one fool at dat stupid lawyer's office."

"Maybe he smart after all," Lucy mumbled.

"Hah? What you said?"

Lucy's eyes exchanged a subtle, knowing glance with Sammy's. "Nothing. I was jus' talkin' to myself."

"Dis bruddah of mine. Nothing can enter his dense brain." Lola took a tumbler from the dish drainer and turned the faucet. The faucet coughed, sputtered, then spat rusty water into the tumbler. "Whas wrong wit' dah water?"

"Clarence was fixing the plumbing. Suppose to bleed the

water pipes. I t'ink he forgot. Jus' run the water fo' little while. Should clear up."

Lola followed her sister's instructions. When the clarity of the water suited her, she drank a couple of glassfuls. Wiping her mouth with a napkin, she continued: "You see. Yo' plan fo' be nice to him backfired."

"But was yo' suggestion," Lucy protested.

"Bettah we take Hank's advice. Jus' take Gilbert to court. Once and fo' all. Get it over wit."

"Hank who?"

"Hank . . . I mean, Mr. Wilkins."

"But—"

"But what?"

"But when you come down to it, dah land really belong to Gilbert. Das what Mama and Papa said to us when dey was living."

"Yeah, das what dey said to us." Glaring. "But you know dey wasn't in dey right mind. Dey tol' us dat jus' befo' dey ma-ke. Really couldn't make dat much sense what dey was talking about."

"What you mean dey wasn't in dey right mind?" Lucy returned, a bit piqued. "I could understand dem. Dey was making sense. Nothin' was wrong wit' what dey was saying."

"What I mean by dat is dat Mama and Papa nevah was thinking 'bout us. We dey children, too. So we get the right to the property, too."

"I still think dey was thinkin' all right. You callin' Mama and Papa stupid?"

"No-no-no," Lola rattled, a bit concerned now that she was losing control of the conversation. "I never mean it like dat. No-no-no. I never said Mama and Papa was crazy. I jus' mean dat was hard to understand dem. You know, ever since Papa got his stroke, and den Mama right after, been hard to understand what dey sayin'."

"But Gilbert always could understand. I could understand."

"I could, too," Lola rebutted. "I could understand dem."

"But how come you said you couldn't understand dem, den?"

"You don't know what I mean. What I mean is dat sometimes it was hard fo' understand dem. Plus, getting back to my original point, dey really wasn't thinkin' about us, you and me, and our families."

"But we get one house and some land already."

"What house? What land? You and I, we live in rat traps!"

"I like dis house."

"No, you dunno what I mean. Dis house is real nice. You made dis one real nice house. What I mean, look how big Mama's and Papa's property, and then compare that wit' what we got. No comparison." She waved her arms emphatically about the kitchen.

"But Mommy, I like our house," Sammy said.

"If I like yo' opinion, I ask fo' it! All right?"

Defeated, Sammy went back to scraping the bottom of his bowl.

"Sammy, you want some more Auntie's stew?" Lucy asked.

Sammy nodded his head.

"Anything fo' my favorite nephew." She took his empty bowl, paddled a mound of rice in it, then ladled stew over the rice.

"Dat land is ours, Lucy. If you like it or not. Not Gilbert's. Dat lolohead, he incompetent. What Hank said was right. We can fight him in court and win. Gilbert is far too gone in dah head to be dah owner of so much land."

"But Gilbert's name is on dah deed," Lucy said, licking the drippings on her fingers. She washed her hands under the faucet stream.

"What name? What deed? Get dah deed, but only get Mama's and Papa's name on dah pepah. Not Gilbert's. All dis time I thought had his name on it, but das not dah case. Hank wen check up fo' me—fo' us—and he said dat only get Mama's and Papa's name on it. So, legally speaking, we get jus' as much right to dah land as Gilbert get."

"You believe in dat haole?" Lucy charged. "Even Papa said befo' he had his bad stroke, he said, 'No let no haole step on dah land.'"

"I t'ink Hank dealing wit' us fair. At least he in his right mind. I t'ink he's one nice man."

Lucy shook her head, then considered the weather again, trying to determine if it was raining in the valley.

"What you squinting at?" Lola asked suspiciously.

"Nothing. Look like it's going to rain."

"Been like dis all day."

"We need the rain."

"It poured last night."

"We need the rain."

The sisters were silent, both watching for no good reason Sammy eating his stew. Sammy looked up, for the kitchen had become suddenly quiet. "Dah stew good, Auntie."

"Just help yo'self, Sammy. Help yo'self. Get plenty rice."

Lola settled on the chair between her son and Lucy. "Dis whole matter is tearing our family apart," Lola sighed.

"Lola . . . we family. Gilbert is our bruddah. Fo' bettah or worse."

"You don't think I know dat? I trying to do dah best fo' dah family's interest. But Gilbert, he's causing all dese problems."

"I like my family dah way it is. I get one good husband. I get good children. We not rich, we not poor. But we happy."

"Easy fo' you say all dis. You get one good husband. You sitting pretty in yo' house."

"But you get one house, too. You get one big check ev'ry month from the gov'ment."

"But where my husband? My husband dead! Gone! At least you get one husband. I get nothing. Only me and Sammy." She took Sammy's arm. Turning to Lucy, she declared, "There's no way in hell I going let Gilbert spoil our chances fo' be rich. And das dat."

THIRTEEN

She was smiling into the telephone, at his warm, deep voice. Closing her eyes, she felt a swelling desire that was oppressing her, making her breathing short and unsteady. His voice was so masculine, so robust, so wonderfully romantic, making her body . . . itchy all over.

"So is that all right with you?" he asked.

"Yes, anything . . ." She was about to say darling but blocked the impulse; it was just too soon to say it, though everything seemed to be falling in its place.

"That's great. So why don't I send my limousine to pick you up, say around six tonight?"

"That would be nice," she crooned.

"Okay, till tonight. At dinner. Bye."

"Bye."

At the drop of the receiver, Wilkins smiled with satisfaction. *I've got that fat woman right around my finger, just where I want her.*

He went out on the balcony of his hotel room and looked over the hotel pool, rubbing his chest, then scratching his scrotum.

A sleepy, woman's voice called from the bedroom. "Hank . . . who did you just talk to?"

A shapely brunette ambled on the pool deck, spreading a beach towel on a chair. Wilkins watched as she lay on her stomach and untied the back straps of her bikini top.

"Hank?"

He broke away from his survey. "Yes, honey?"

"Who was that on the phone?"

"Oh, I had to contact a business associate. We have to meet over dinner tonight."

"Hon, how about coming back in here?"

He took one last look at the woman by the pool, then turned away, sliding shut the glass door to keep the cool air in. Padding back to the artificial darkness of the bedroom, he slipped into bed next to the waiting woman.

FOURTEEN

Nakakura-san and Gilbert were moseying along the road when the old man noticed something shiny on the ground. He stopped to pick it up. It was a foil wrapper from a stick of chewing gum.

"You see, Gilbert. Dah signs."

"What kine signs?"

"Dah signs dat dah frogmen still around. You gotta be careful."

Gilbert was going to say that his sister might have tossed the wrapper out of her car window—she was always chewing on something—but he decided to remain quiet.

Nakakura-san scanned the sky, then stared at the rising morning sun. Gilbert looked too, but the sun was too strong for him. He looked away, the sun blinding his vision.

"What you looking fo', Uncle-san?" he asked, rubbing his eyes.

The old man didn't answer, his unblinking eyes staring at the sun. Then a buzzing sound came from Nakakura-san. The old man tottered forward a step or two, backward a few steps, and collapsed to the ground.

"Uncle-san! Uncle-san!" Gilbert hurried to the old man's side and propped up his head.

"Ho—dizzy—I feel dizzy—"

"Uncle-san!! Whassamattah?"

"Gilbert—I t'ink dis is it."

"What you mean? No say dat! No say dat, Uncle-san!"

"Gilbert—you no see dah signs—in dah sky? Dey coming again—ho—I tired already—chase dem away—Save Waipuna—Gilbert—you gotta chase 'em away—now—By yo'self—Only you know—"

"But what signs? Where?"

"Deah." Weakly, he pointed to the sky. "Deah."

"Where?"

"Deah."

Gilbert searched the sky but couldn't see anything. "Where?"

"Gilbert!—I gotta paint—one picture—fo' you everytime?—You stupid—o' what?—Deah!—Dah cloud—You no see—dah cloud—how stay look—like one frog?"

He looked at the cloud that was slowly expanding. No, it didn't look like a frog. It looked like . . . a cloud. But Gilbert nodded his head.

"Das—dah sign—of dah frogmen—Look 'em—Das dah sign—Dat mean—dey coming back—dis time—wit' mo' force—

The WATCHER *of* WAIPUNA **67**

Watch out, Gilbert—Get ready—"

The old man smiled for a long, lavishing moment, then frowned.

"Whas wrong, Uncle-san?"

"Gilbert—I get plenny—trust in you—agh!—dat you—dat you—dat you do—one good job—But remembah—dis—" The old man pressed a hand to his chest. "Remembah dis—Gilbert—dat we only dah—dah small kine Watcher—Dah Big Watcher—das dah one—das dah one who really—run dah show—Respect him—"

"Dah big—?"

"Dah Big Watcher—Respect him!"

"Who's dah Big Watcher?"

"Banzai . . . banzai . . . ban—"

His eyes rolled, then closed. His body tightened, shook for a few moments, then relaxed. A smile came to his face, but that slowly faded.

Gilbert didn't know what to do. He burst into tears and cried for several minutes. Then, respectfully, he carried his mentor's body to the side of the road and placed it on a tuft of grass and weeds, under the shade of a mango tree. He regarded the cloud again, which had now formed into a pig's head—he could plainly see that—and then regarded the old man's placid, graying face. He drew in a deep breath. Now he, Gilbert Sanchez, was the Watcher of Waipuna. Period. Whatever that meant. All he knew was that the frogmen were still around and getting ready for another attack. But where were they now and what were they going to attack? The old man had told him that the frogmen were very tricky, that they could attack from anywhere, at anytime. That's how tricky they were.

A chill went through Gilbert. He looked at the mountain range, at Mr. Nascimento's banana patch, down the road towards his house, towards the direction of the village, then back to the old man's face. He, Gilbert Sanchez, was the Watcher of Waipuna, whether he liked it or not. And that was the hard truth of the matter. He surveyed his surroundings again and, with a sigh, made a pledge to the people of Waipuna—and to himself—to do the best job that he could as the newly installed Watcher of Waipuna.

He went into the Nascimento banana patch, cut three large leaves, then returned and covered the old man's body. He prayed silently for a minute. Then he picked up the old man's walking stick and headed towards the village for help.

FIFTEEN

Lucy Bitten's conscience bothered her so much that she decided to visit Gilbert secretly one night and tell all.

Early one evening, after Lola and Sammy had gone back home, she went to the Catholic church to pray and confess her sins; and upon leaving the church, she experienced something which she believed to be a Sign of Grace: a mynah bird, sleeping in the rafters over the entrance, did a nocturnal emission, spotting Lucy as she paused below to open her umbrella. Though momentarily disgusted, in the next instant she became engrossed in the significance of that wet emblem. She decided right then and there to make amends with Gilbert.

It was drizzling in the village, and halfway down the coastal road a storm erupted. Heavy rains came down, so hard in fact that Lucy almost turned back. But her conscience pushed her onward. She needed to tell Gilbert everything. Then—and only then—would her conscience be free.

About a mile before the house her car stalled. She turned the engine over at least a dozen times before the weakening battery gave up. Cursing, she got out of the car with her umbrella and plodded through the rain and mud towards the house. It was a short distance away, but the rain made visibility near nil and the wind made her weave, even though she was built like a buoy. Finally she reached the short concrete bridge, which was about three hundred yards before the house. The stream under it had risen to just about the height of the banks.

As Lucy crossed the bridge, holding precariously to the guardrail, a flash flood was rolling down from the highlands, picking up a mountain of momentum. Hearing this growing rumble, she paused. Moments later, a mountain of water slammed into the bridge. The bridge buckled, and Lucy was thrown into the guardrail on the other side. If it weren't for her size and the narrow spacing of the railing, the water would have swept her to sea. Instead, she lay unconscious, an arm and leg dangling over the side of the bridge.

SIXTEEN

Lola was looking out the large picture window of the steakhouse. "Oooh," she cooed, "it's raining."

Things weren't going the way she hoped they would. All Hank had talked about so far was the property and the plans of its development. She expected an evening of champagne and dancing . . . and perhaps . . . . Even her New York steak wasn't the way she wanted it; she had ordered it well done and it had come rare.

"Does it rain a lot in Waipuna?" Wilkins asked.

"I guess more than other places."

"According to a survey that we had commissioned, Waipuna's beaches are considered the best on the island by locals."

"Oh, we got the best beaches." Her eyes drifted to a table across the room where a couple was holding hands. "But ohhh . . . the rain. It's coming down so hard. Maybe I should stay in town tonight. Could be kind of dangerous to drive home."

"Let the chauffeur worry about that. He'll get you anywhere you want to go, under the most adverse conditions."

"You know, I don't have to be anywhere tonight."

Wilkins labored at a smile. "By the way, we haven't really talked about how all this will affect your brother, of course in a positive way."

"Oh, I don't want to talk about my brother. He's going to be taken care of."

"Oh. You already have plans for him?"

"My sister. She's so concerned about him. So I'm going to let her take care of him."

"Oh, that's really nice of her. And speaking about your sister—"

"Oh, the hell with her."

"Excuse me?"

"I said the hell with my sister."

"And why is that?"

"She's not interested in making money. She's too concerned about my retarded brother."

"Oh, I see. Well, I don't really see that as a problem."

"But it is because she doesn't want to be involved in all of this legal matter any more."

"You mean she doesn't want to contest the property rights?"

"Yes."

"Well, this can be a problem. The suit we have pending is on behalf of you and your sister. If your sister's unwilling, I can foresee a real problem."

"Oh, but don't worry about that. My kid sister always listens to whatever I tell her."

"Then it'll be no problem?"

"No . . . no problem."

"Well, I hope that solves that. If this complication can be ironed out, then I don't see how anything can stop us—stop you and your sister, that is—from getting your proper and fair share of the revenue. You'll be richly rewarded, I can assure you."

Lola tried to join his eyes with hers but was unsuccessful. Uncomfortable by her stare, Wilkins pushed his plate of gristle and blood to the side and motioned for the waiter.

"I never visited any of the rooms in this hotel before," she said. "Is it beautiful, the rooms?"

"Why—uh—they're all right."

"What color is your room?"

"Oh, I don't know. I don't pay attention to that kind of thing. It's been a busy week for me and Jerre. Waiter!"

"Didn't you say Jerre had to leave?"

"Yes, to a neighbor island, but he'll be back tomorrow on the early morning flight. Excuse me, Lola."

He got up and went to the waiter's station. "Make it fast," he ordered, giving the waiter a credit card. "I'm expecting an important business call."

Back at the table, he forced another smile. "Well, I guess everything is rolling now. The court date is in two weeks. And don't worry. We'll take care of everything. We'll send the limousine to pick up you and your sister."

"Hank . . . do you dance?"

"Oh, no. I'm not a good dancer. Well, it was a nice dinner, wasn't it? I think we've accomplished a lot tonight. What do you think?"

"Hank, can I ask you a personal question?"

"Sure."

"Are you married?"

"Well—I—uh—I was. I got divorced three years ago."

"Oh."

"Well, I'll tell the driver to be real careful on the way home. We don't want you to have an accident, do we? It was a nice dinner and I enjoyed myself immensely. I'm sorry I have to cut this evening short, but I have an awfully busy schedule tomorrow and I'm expecting a phone call from the mainland in a short while. Oh, here comes the check. Boy, do they want us out of here."

Lola watched Wilkins sign the charge slip. She thought how cute he was when flustered. He must be the shy type, she decided, but that was all right. Actually, she liked the type. And now that she had tossed out the net, she gave herself two days to pull it in with that big mullet.

SEVENTEEN

Gilbert was on his nightly patrol when he heard a moaning from the bridge. He crossed himself, nervously uttered a Hail Mary, then gripped Nakakura-san's walking stick tightly. He crept towards the moans. The rain was coming down steady, though not as heavy as earlier. Before stepping on the bridge, he directed the beam of his powerful flashlight across it. The light found an odd, dark form about midpoint across. Whatever it is, Gilbert thought, it's trying to climb up. His heart pounded. He swallowed hard. He stepped back, but the image of the old man and himself battling the flying frogmen came to him, filling him with purpose. Raising the stick and giving a loud "Banzai," he rushed forward.

Luckily for Lucy, Gilbert slipped and fell on his face, the

falling stick missing her head by inches.

Scrambling up, Gilbert was about to strike again when he blinked, then shielded his eyes from the blurring rain. It was what he thought he saw. What the hell was Lucy doing sleeping on the bridge in the middle of a storm?

"Lucy!" He touched her cold face. She moaned. "Lucy—what you doing here? You all right?" He could see that she wasn't all right. He shook her, which aggravated her moans. Carrying her on his back, he brought her to the house.

Covered with an old army blanket, Lucy opened her eyes to a concerned and watchful Gilbert. She choked on her saliva. Coughing, she felt a sharp pain on her side. When she recovered, she looked again at Gilbert, who was now offering her something warm to drink. She began to cry.

Gilbert was shaken. What had come over Lucy? Was there a death in the family?

"Lucy! Whassamattah?"

But Lucy, in her uncontrollable storm of tears and guilt, was too lost to answer. Finally, after ten minutes of sobbing, she dried her eyes and turned to Gilbert, though avoiding any eye contact. "Gilbert," she began, her voice small and withered, "dey coming to take dah land away from you."

Gilbert looked as calm as the eye of a storm. Raising his bushy, graying eyebrows, he said, "Yeah, I know."

She eyed him cautiously. "You heard what I said?"

"Yeah. But I know dat already, dat dey coming here." Gilbert demonstrated his readiness by raising the stick above his head in mock attack form.

Lucy gawked, covering her face with the blanket. "No—Gilbert! Wasn't me! Wasn't me!"

He lowered the stick, his eyebrows frowning. "I sorry I got you scared. I was jus' showing you how ready I am as . . . dah Watcher."

Lucy lowered the blanket. Gilbert offered her the cup of tea again. She shook her head.

"Gilbert—I—I jus' like say I sorry all dis thing wen happen.

Das why I came over here tonight, to tell you whas going on, what dah men are saying, what dey going do."

"You wen talk to dah frogmen?" A look of alarm and disbelief came to Gilbert's face. "Wen you talked to dem? Where?"

"She wen what? Talk—to dah—dah—dah—frogmen?" Gilbert the drinker stammered.

"Dah what men? Dah frogmen?"

The lights flickered, then went out. Gilbert groped into the kitchen and returned with a kerosene lantern, setting it on the table next to Lucy. "Ho . . . dis storm is bad news," he said. "Yeah, dah frogmen. You wen talk to dem?"

Thinking Gilbert meant the attorney, James Fogarty, she nodded her head guiltily. "Yeah, Gilbert, we wen talk to him." She looked up, her reddened eyes wide and begging for forgiveness. "But I never like sign nothing. Promise, Gilbert. Lola the one wen force me to the meeting. I never wen sign nothing. You know me, I would never sign nothing over to dem. Not from my own will. Promise."

"Sign what?"

"You know. Dah law suit."

"Dah law suit?" Gilbert was confused.

"But I had to sign. And I know dey like you sign, too. But I came here tonight to tell you about dis." She paused. "And also to ask you fo'—fo'—fo' fo'giveness."

"You wen talk to dem and dey wen make you dah Sign . . ." Gilbert mused.

"Dey like dah land."

He grinned with understanding. "Jus' like how Uncle-san wen say. He knew all along, dat old man."

"What you mean?" Lucy asked.

"Dah frogmen. Dey coming to take dah land. Gotta protect Waipuna."

"What you talking about, Gilbert?"

He straightened himself and declared, as if addressing an audience, "I dah new Watcher of Waipuna."

Believing her brother had finally gone off the deep end, she thought fast and asked him for a cup of tea. Gilbert gave her the one he had offered, but after a sip she told him that the tea was too cold. And while Gilbert was in the kitchen heating water on the gas stove, she snuck to the telephone to call Lola. But the phone lines, too, were down. Cursing, she returned to the sofa.

Gilbert brought the hot tea. He was smiling.

"Lucy, I get one good plan," he said. "You said you saw dah Sign. Eh, I saw dah Sign, too. Eh, das good. We both saw dah Sign. Dat means both of us gotta do something about it. So, because of dat fact, I going deputize you as my assistant. You going be dah Assistant Watcher."

"Dah *what?* Assistant to *what?*"

"Dah Assistant Watcher of Waipuna."

"Assistant . . . *Watcher?* Gilbert, what you talking about?"

"I get one plan," Gilbert continued. "Indications is dat dey going come soon. Maybe even tonight. Who knows. So you and me, we gotta be ready. We gotta stay hiding wit' our sticks. And when dey come, we jump out and clobber dey heads."

Lucy covered her gasp. "Gilbert, you taking 'bout murder."

"No. I talking how we going save Waipuna from dah frogmen, jus' like how Uncle-san said I gotta do."

"Gilbert, you can take me home?"

"Yeah. But wait. Listen to what I get to say."

So Gilbert told his plan, about how he and Lucy would have to dig into the underground limestone caves. Then they would have to wait in hiding under the bridge until the frogmen passed over them, whereupon they would come out and attack the frogmen with their sticks and chase them toward the holes. Falling into the limestone caves, the frogmen would be eaten by the blind mullets, thus getting rid of them once and for all.

Lucy was speechless. A chill came over her. Was she having a nightmare? She pinched herself. Should she call the police and have her brother arrested before he went out and did something crazy? So absorbed was she in the horror of Gilbert's scheme, she had to be shaken five times before realizing that Gilbert had changed the subject from the frogmen to his taking her home. With her senses numb, she nodded and took their mother's raincoat that Gilbert was offering.

"Gilbert, you better really t'ink dis out . . . what you tol' me right now," she said shakily.

"What I tol' you right now?"

"About . . . about hurting all dose people."

"I not trying hurt anybody, but I like get dem buggahs, dose frogs."

"Frogs?"

"Yeah. I not going hurt nobody. Jus' dem buggahs. Dose frogmen."

"Who are dose frogmen? What dey look like?"

Gilbert couldn't answer the question, since he really didn't know how they looked. So he changed the subject, asking her if she was ready to leave. He led Lucy to the leaky garage where their father's ancient Ford truck, undriven for five years, was parked.

"Look at Papa's truck," he said. "Wen was the last time you rode in it?"

"You been keeping up Papa's truck?"

"No. Dah truck not running."

"But how you going drive me home in dis truck in dis rain, den, if not working?"

"I not going drive dah truck, but you going ride dah truck."

The enigma of the answer dulled Lucy. She climbed into the driver's seat and released the handbrakes, following her brother's instructions.

"What you going do, Gilbert? How you going get dis truck fo' move?"

"I going push."

"You going what?"

"Push. You know, push dah car."

"Push dah car? In dah rain?"

"Yeah. Das dah only way I know how get you home wit'out you getting all wet."

"But you going get wet . . . and my house is five miles away."

Gilbert smiled. "Das all right. I get wet all dah time. But you my sistah. I cannot let you get wet. Especially wen you hurt. C'mon, steer dah car. First, we going yo' car, see if can fix 'em." He gave her a flashlight to help her see through the windshield, but in the thick rain it was of no use.

She closed her eyes and shook her head. How could her brother be so stupid? She heard Gilbert grunting and felt the truck lurch forward but go nowhere. Then she realized that the transmission was in gear. So she released the clutch and shifted it into neutral. The truck left the gauzy air of the garage and entered the rain. Panicking since her vision was now blurred, Lucy jammed the brakes.

"Eh! What you doing?" Gilbert hollered.

Lucy rolled down the window. "I no can see! Dah rain blinding me!"

"Try use dis handle." Gilbert pointed to the knob of a makeshift manual wiper that his father had devised when the mechanical one broke down fifteen years ago. "Jus' turn 'em wit' yo' hand and dah blades going move."

She sighed but did what Gilbert suggested. The knob was hard to turn, but it got easier when rain got into the mechanism, lubricating it.

The truck trundled the three hundred yards or so to the bridge, then a bit further to Lucy's stalled vehicle. Gilbert tinkered with the ignition, and miraculously the car started. Running the car for about five minutes, he then jump-started the truck.

Lucy thanked him, planting a kiss on a cold wet cheek, then got into her car and drove off, leaving a dripping Gilbert smiling from that kiss.

It wasn't until she entered a temporary lull in the storm about halfway home—when her thoughts weren't drummed by the rain on the car's roof—did she come to a realization that Gilbert had done one of the kindest things that anyone had ever done for her. It warmed her heart and her eyes started to tear. A minute later, the wind and rain returned, and the car began to weave again.

While wiping her eyes, she misnegotiated a turn onto the short wooden bridge over Waipuna Stream. The car broke through the guardrails and plunged sideways into the water. The rushing stream righted the car, then lodged it against the bank.

When Lucy regained consciousness, she saw a mass of unblinking eyes on her. Having been swept down from their highland homes by the sudden torrent, hundreds of frogs had found a refuge in Lucy's car, escaping the churning waters and an inevitable death at sea.

Lucy thought she was dead. Her body was wrinkled and numb from the cold water. Fortunately, with the car tilted to the back, the headrest had kept her head above water, preventing her from drowning.

A small frog, inches from her face, emitted a tiny ribbit. She screamed and thrashed the water, and the frogs dispersed to hiding places throughout the car.

EIGHTEEN

Miraculously, Lucy came out of the accident with only a bruised thigh and a challenged heart. But it was a cleansed heart, without a trace of guilt or regret. She had finally taken a stand, even if it was against her big sister, and it was done with the deepest concern for the family. She knew now that her sister was wrong—morally, spiritually, maybe even legally—for she believed that her sister had been swayed by forces, perhaps dark forces, which, as she was beginning to conclude, had tried to kill her. But the Almighty was truly merciful and had forgiven her for her sins; and reconciling with her family spirits had probably given her additional protection against a fatal outcome. An escape from death could only be interpreted as an auspicious portent.

The morning after the accident, Lucy had her eldest son drive her to town. With the help of a cane, she hobbled into the lawyer's office and demanded that her name be removed from the documents. The skeptical lawyer shook his head and said, "No."

"What do you mean?" Lucy demanded.

"Simply, the motion has been filed," the lawyer said. "There's nothing I or anyone else can do. There's nothing we can argue about."

"What motion? What you talking about? So what dis means?"

"This means that you and your sister can just sit back and

wait, for both of you are going to be very rich ladies in a short while. Filthy rich."

"What you mean by all dis? What kine pepahs you wen file?"

"Didn't your sister tell you? Both of you are suing your brother. And, as your attorney, I can assure you that the case against him is absolutely foolproof."

"I don't want to be filthy rich. I want my name off dah pepah!" Lucy struck the top of the lawyer's desk with the walking stick.

"Mrs. Bitten . . . please. Let me explain—"

"No! I want you explain nothin' to me! I had enough of all dis explaining bullshit!"

"Mrs. Bitten . . . please, please sit down. Let's talk this out."

"I said I don't want to talk about it!"

"Mama, calm down—"

"Shut up, Lyle! Eh—you,"—to the attorney—"you not trying to help us out. You doing dis so you can get yo' big cut of dah pie. Don't give me all dah bullshit. You don't care about my family falling apart, you goddamn, nogood friggin'—"

"Mrs. Bitten, please control yourself. This is a law office, and I have clients waiting outside."

"I don't really give a shit about yo' clients or you."

"I will ask you again to control yourself."

"I'm going to control you wit' dis stick." She raised her stick to strike the attorney, but was quickly restrained by her son.

"Mama! Mama! Whachu doing?"

"Stay back, Lyle! Stay back!"

"Mama! Put dah stick down!"

The lawyer smiled across his desk, though obviously shaken. He picked up the phone, ready to press a digit. "I'm sorry, Mrs. Bitten, but if you don't vacate the premises right this moment, I'm calling the police."

"I going to vacate yo' ugly head!" She squirmed out of Lyle's grip and swung at the attorney, missing him but batting the telephone to the floor.

"That's it! That's it!" the attorney shrieked. "Judy! Judy!

Call the police! Judy!"

"Mama! Les go. He going call dah cops."

Spouting all of the most un-Christian Anglo-Saxon words brought to the islands by God-fearing New England whalers, Lucy fought with Lyle as he wrestled her out of the office. She raised her cane to smash the glass door, but was blocked by Lyle's quick hands, an inherent talent of his which was largely responsible for his selection to the All-State defensive backfield in his junior year of high school.

"I going get dem," Lucy said bitterly. "Even if I haf' to die trying."

"Mama—whachu saying?!"

"Nevah mind. Dese buggahs, dey like cheat us from our land. I had one hunch. But yo' dumb auntie—she so blind. All she can t'ink of is how handsome dat friggin' haole is. And dah buggah is so ugly!"

Lyle was going to ask again what she was talking about, but he decided to remain silent, a trait he had inherited from his father.

"I knew all along. Why I nevah do something about it? Now too late."

They waited to cross the main street, while she mumbled repeatedly, "Now too late." Two cars passed, then Lyle helped his mother off the curb and walked her towards their car. But in the middle of the street, Lucy noticed something that stopped her. It was a dead toad, flattened by a car and dried to a crisp by the sun and the hot asphalt.

Lyle tugged at her arm, but she resisted. "Mama, c'mon. Befo' dah cars run us ovah."

Lucy didn't care about the cars, she was stunned by an insight. "Dah frogs," she muttered. "We hide. Den come out. Den smash 'em, smash 'em all. Das dah plan. What a good plan."

"Mama . . . whachu talking about?"

"Dah frogs."

Then Lucy hobbled off to the car, not wasting another moment and leaving Lyle back at the smashed toad worrying that perhaps the accident had bruised more than his mother's thigh.

She instructed Lyle to drive directly to his uncle's house. Entering Waipuna Village, they heard thunderous, earth-shaking sounds. Halfway down Waipuna's main and only street, they spotted a large battalion of trucks and tractors and cranes, all methodically grinding and buzzing through the drowsy village, their tires leaving muddy tracks on the broken macadam. Several residents were out watching the event, their faces drawn and possessed with a silence, as if the construction company were an army of occupation.

Lyle drove past the Nakakura Store, but Lucy ordered him to turn back and stop there.

"Jimson, what dah hell is going on over here?" Lucy asked as she entered the store.

The storekeeper shrugged his shoulders. "I dunno. But all dat noise when shake dah corn flakes off dah top shelf."

"Who was dat, dah developers?"

He offered his shoulders again.

"Holy Moses!" She sat down on an empty crate marked "California Cantaloupes." "Lyle, get me one orange soda and get what you like fo' yo'self."

Jimson deliberately refolded the morning newspaper, which he was browsing through for the fourth time that afternoon, and watched the boy open the red cooler, take out two bottles and uncap them.

"You going drink heah?" Jimson asked. Lucy told him they were. "Twenty-five cents plus twenty-five cents . . . fifty cents, altogether."

"Lyle, you got money? I left my bag in the car."

The boy took out the exact change from his pocket and paid the storekeeper.

"Look like we too late," Lucy said, sighing. She looked out the door, then turned to the display of cellophane-packaged dried cuttle fish and preserved Chinese plums. Next to the display was a poster advertising the coming of the E. K. Fernandez Circus to Town. Jimson returned to the newspaper.

Lucy stared out the doorway again and saw a toad hop lazily under her car for shade. She watched the toad for a while, finished her soda and said, "No, not too late." Depositing the empty bottle in the wire receptacle next to the door, she hobbled past Lyle. "Hurry up, son, les go. Or pay dah five cents deposit."

They drove down the coastal road for several miles, and right before the bridge they came across the area where the trucks, tractors and cranes were parked. The drivers were in a van, waiting to be transported back to Town. Lyle slowed down as they surveyed the extent of the land that had been cleared for the equipment. Lucy waved him on.

Gilbert was not at home, so they waited. For a long time. Until the sun set behind the mountains. Just as they were about to leave, Gilbert came strutting up the driveway.

Lucy hurried to him as fast as she could. "Gilbert! Gilbert!"

Gilbert slowed, smiled with surprise, then waved the guava stick in greeting. Brother and sister embraced.

"Gilbert, I get lots to talk to you about."

"Whassamattah wit' yo' leg?"

"Nevah mind 'bout dat. You notice anything strange going on around here?"

"Yeah. You saw all dat down deah?" he said, pointing down the road.

"Yeah. Dah frogs," Lucy said.

"Dah what?"

"Dah frogs. I mean, dah frogmen."

"Whachu talking about?" An alarm came to his face.

"Dah frogmen all parked in dah land cleared away," Lucy stated.

"You mean dah trucks and tractors?"

"Yeah-yeah," Lucy said, nodding her head. "Dah trucks and tractors, whatevahs. Dah frogmen."

Baffled, Gilbert asked, "But where you saw dah frogmen?"

Lucy rolled her eyes. "Right deah. Dah trucks and tractors like dat, das dah frogmen. Gilbert, das dah frogmen you was talking about."

"Dah frogmen? Dah frogmen no look like dat." Then he

remembered the cloud that Nakakura-san had brought to his attention, how it had changed to another size and shape. Grinning with new understanding, he said, "Yeah, I think you right. I think you right, Lucy."

"So what we going do?"

"Who?"

"Me and you. What we going do?"

"I dunno. What we should do?"

"What about dah plan you tol' me dah other night, last night—what about dat?"

Gilbert couldn't remember the plan. So Lucy repeated it to him.

"Sounds good to me," he said. "And Lyle, he going be part of dah plan?"

Lucy looked at her son who was regarding them cautiously from the bottom of the porch steps. "Yeah," she said, "him, too. Because of him, das why I doing all of dis."

NINETEEN

Strange things started happening in Waipuna.

For one, it poured for three days straight. It rained so hard that the residents could not get out of their homes. After the deluge, they finally got out, surveyed the damage and were relieved to find that outside of minor water damage to homes and businesses, nothing really catastropic had happened. But they did find the flooded main street swarming with hundreds of thousands of squirmy tadpoles. Said Clarence Bitten to his eldest son Lyle, "I no think I evah thought I was going evah see dis happen in my lifetime, in yo' lifetime fo' dat mattah. But dis is bad stuff when it rain tadpoles." He related a story told to him by his grandmother a time long ago about the last time Waipuna had had a rain of frogs. For months it had brought bad things to the valley. Taro patches rotted, schools of dead fish covered the beach and mothers miscarried a generation. The people asked a kahuna to bless the valley, but it wasn't until after the next big rain—a long, long wait—when the frogs vanished as mysteriously as they had appeared.

The sun stayed for the next several days, beating down and evaporating the ponds and puddles of rain, and though a lot of the tadpoles had instinctively found their way to the streams and ponds, a lot more were stranded on the drying land. Soon the air of Waipuna became addled with the smell of rotting gelatin.

Months later, while the workmen were clearing the land near the Sanchezes' homestead and getting ready to plow over their barbed wire fence, the underground limestone caves were being discovered—or rather, the trucks and tractors were finding the ground under them unable to support their enormous weight. In one day alone, five tractors and three trucks had fallen into uselessness. The company had to call a heavy-duty tow truck from Honolulu, which took an entire day to arrive since it had blown a tire on the way, and when it finally came and started to pull out its first load, the ground under it caved in, and it too was incapacitated. Another tow truck came four days later, and this time workers used a long steel cable to free the vehicles. Meanwhile, half of the work force had quit; word had gone around that heavy-handed spirits were enforcing their jurisdiction over the area. Another quarter of the men considered leaving, or pretended illness, while the other quarter were too dumb or too cynical to be bothered by this scenario of soothsayers.

Another thing happened.

Charlie the mailman was the first to see it. He was driving down the coastal road, returning home from another long day at work, when he saw a ball of bright light flash across the road in front of him. Startled, he pulled over to the side. When he got back on the road, he found that his headlights had gone off. He tried to turn the lights back on but succeeded only in breaking the switch. With the hairs on the back of his neck standing on end, he drove the rest of the way home in the dark, his eyes wide as moons. Next morning he discovered both of his headlights burnt out.

That same night, Jimson Nakakura was closing up the store when he saw his father straggling behind a line of ghosts lumbering down the main street. Others saw the marchers, too. Sonny Boy DeCosta swore he saw them when returning home after a night of torch fishing, though Sonny's friends refused to verify his testimony.

Donald Nascimento was also heading down the coastal road, having delivered a truckload of bananas to markets in Town. As he made a tight turn in the road, he barely missed driving through the last of the marchers. He screeched to a stop and made a 180-degree turn, fishtailed on the grassy shoulder, then blazed back to the village. On a straightaway, his speedometer clocked the speed of forty-seven miles an hour, an amazing feat for a small pickup with only three cylinders working. Donald told himself that he did not see what he had seen; but then again, not believing what he was telling himself, he decided that the best thing to do was to spend the night at his sister's house on the other side of the village.

In the meantime, Hawaiian International Corporation was adding loss on top of loss. After more than five months of futility and headaches (its Japanese partners had decided to bail out, giving the first three months of troubles as their excuse, though compounded more by the publication of a series of articles in a local paper exposing the head of the Japanese Imperial Bank as having "undisputedly shady" connections with the Japanese underworld), and after a loss in excess of 37 million dollars in damaged equipment and wages and lost time and mounting interest payments to the banks, the company folded operations and filed for Chapter Seven, leaving as its last testament four-and-a-half acres of cleared land.

TWENTY

One afternoon, two months after Hawaiian International's foreclosure, Gilbert returned home from a day's fishing to a yard full of small frogs. Spellbound by that sea of amphibians, he dropped the bucket of blind mullet at his feet. He didn't know what to do. Then he remembered the power of the old man's walking stick and raced into the house to get it, his wide feet flattening frogs along the way. But he couldn't find the stick that he had placed next to the telephone; it was lost somewhere in a house full of frogs. Horrified, he fled the house, screaming, "DAH FROGS COMING! DAH FROGS COMING!" He ran down the road, determined to warn the village of the danger. "DAH FROGS HEAH! DAH FROGS HEAH!"

He ran until his heart and lungs just about gave up, and, on the road next to the Nascimento banana patch, he collapsed, almost at the exact spot on which old man Nakakura had collapsed and died. Fearing that history just might repeat itself, he struggled up—even with his heart throbbing in pain, his lungs on fire and his mouth tasting of blood—and ran like a madman all the way to the village without stopping.

For the SAKE of a CHRIST

Josie Nakahara had described the baby as having the head of a German shepherd. Her friends on the bowling team agreed with her, except for Harriet Robello, who said the baby reminded her of a hyena. And Gerdy Ching, who ran the corner grocery store, made a comment to her wheelchair-ridden husband that the DeSilva baby had looked more like one of those long-nosed monkeys she had seen on a National Geographic special. The most discrepant description came from Mrs. Winona Carlson, the weak-sighted, eighty-nine-year-old, pure-blooded Hawaiian lady who lived in the second house on the right, past the Chings' convenience store; she suggested that the baby was a cross between man and shark.

The strangest thing about it all was that none of them had ever seen Marianne DeSilva's baby.

The only person in the community who was closest to having actually seen the baby outside of the immediate DeSilva family was Matthew Thom, whose sister was a delivery nurse at the downtown hospital where Marianne DeSilva had given birth. Rapture Chun had told her brother that the baby had been born with big floppy ears, like a beagle's, and she had sworn on the Book that the baby had also a long thin hairy tail. Though the only time Rapture had seen the infant was through two glass doors, the gossip from Thelma Evans, who worked the midnight shift, affirmed her suspicion that the baby was born more animal than human. She had also told Matthew that the baby was born with fiery blue eyes and that its nose was long and dark, sort of hairy. All of this was told to Matthew with his promise that he would tell no one. Matthew later told his wife that the DeSilva baby was born with a face like an anteater. The next day, Eva Thom told her neighbor Harriet Robello that the baby looked like a hyena, and when Harriet said, "What dat look like?" Eva told her that a hyena was the African equivalent of "one wild, mangy kine dog." Later that day, Harriet unraveled her interpretation of the story to the shock of the members of her bowling team; she stated emphatically that Marianne DeSilva must have done it with a German shepherd. And so on and on.

Several months preceding the baby's coming, Marianne's pregnancy was the main talk of the town, for no one knew who the father was, not even Marianne DeSilva. And being that Marianne was beginning her senior year in high school, the talk in the grapevine became more scandalous. Never mind the fact that Gerdy Ching's daughter was pregnant at fifteen and had to give up the baby for adoption, or Harriet Robello's son and Clarence and Jackie Cabugan's daughter were forced to marry right after graduating from high school, or the Thom's unmarried daughter had two daughters from two different guys, or . . .

It didn't help, too, that most of the womenfolk didn't care for Marianne DeSilva's mother, Gloria Clinger DeSilva, who was arrogant and proud of her family roots, even though the Clinger family had lost their money and land and the splendor of their name when Gloria's father went bankrupt on account of several bad investments. Jealousy, too, may have had a lot to do with the town's women despising her; for at forty-five, Gloria DeSilva still had the best figure of her generation, a fact that was given proof beyond proof whenever smiling Gloria passed a grinning husband in town.

In contrast to her mother, Marianne was a sweetheart. She was soft-spoken and never said anything unless she was called upon in class, and even then, she would softly utter only four or five words at a time. She had very few friends, but the friends she had were nice to her and included her in all their activities. She was the total opposite of her mother.

When the story leaked out from St. Anselm's Hospital that the baby was born a freak, the more vocal enemies of Gloria DeSilva began fanning the flames. And soon the winds of gossip even picked up the thoughts and voices of the reticent members of the community; the tempest rose and began to batter the DeSilva household. There circulated a story that the DeSilva family must have done some unforgivable sin and the baby was God's way of punishing them.

Marianne DeSilva didn't know who the father of the infant was. In fact, she never knew of her own pregnancy until she was well into her fourth month. She never had morning sickness; she had what could be called a "good" pregnancy. She had gone to her doctor complaining about missing periods and a swelling and tenderness of her breasts, and when the doctor had quietly informed her of her condition, she lapsed into shock. It was a full five minutes before the doctor could revive her. She had never slept with anyone for at least six or seven months, the last time being on a sultry evening in a deserted State park in the back seat of her boyfriend's Ford Mustang. It was a night she remembered well, for her boyfriend, Jesse Costella, who had been drafted weeks earlier, was to leave for boot camp the following morning. (He would later be shipped off to Vietnam and would come back home—exactly one year, seven months, three weeks and one day later—in a body bag.) Then she remembered the time when she reluctantly had gone with her friends Dory Nakahara and Janice Kamaka to a beach party where, depressed by the departure of her boyfriend and his unresponsiveness in letter writing, she had gotten very drunk. Had she slept with someone there while drunk out of her mind? Had she been raped and had she been so senseless that she could not remember? But the party had occurred at the beginning of the summer, one month before being told of her pregnancy, and the doctor had told her that she could expect delivery within five months, though he could not pinpoint the exact date.

At first she went into a period of acute depression. She ate very little, barely surviving on a diet of soda crackers and water, hoping that somehow she could starve away the pregnancy. And her mother didn't talk to her for a week. Marianne thought of an abortion, but—the DeSilvas being staunch Catholics—that was quickly dismissed. Then she went into a period of voracious craving for anything raw: raw fish, raw crab, raw shellfish (especially 'opihi, which was hard to get). Even raw beef. For the rest of her pregnancy she could not stand the sight of cooked meat. And it became a necessity to smother the raw foods generously with Hawaiian salt.

  It was about the seventh month of the pregnancy when people began to take notice of a thin young man frequenting the DeSilva house. No one in the community knew who he was. He would come in the late afternoon, holding a small guitar by the neck, sometimes carrying gifts wrapped in shiny green or blue paper. He was always neatly dressed and his hair was short and combed but had that wet look as if he had just taken a shower. In the early evenings, he could be heard playing his flatly tuned instrument. Though he carried himself pleasantly and from a distance had an honest look, almost a meek look—the look of an altar boy, as Harriet Robello remarked—the community passed immediate judgment on him, accusing him of being the father of the unborn child. But it was a judgment that was touched with concern for Marianne; though they disliked the mother, most of the community had an affinity for the daughter. They began to develop a strange respect for the young man since he seemed to be taking responsibility for his wrongdoing. But with the baby's birth, the young man stopped coming. And when it was subsequently discovered that the baby was born a freak, the community came to the conclusion that that probably had scared the young man away. Word soon spread that the DeSilva family was cursed, and with this in mind, they decided, upon the suggestion of the bowling league's president Candance Kim, to cancel the annual banquet so that they wouldn't have to go through the inconvenience and embarrassment of not inviting the family of the past president, the late Herman DeSilva.

  A few weeks after the baby's birth, Matthew and Eva Thom saw the young man waiting at a city bus stop. They were anxious at first, but dying curiosity made them approach him and ask him about the baby and why he had stopped going over to the DeSilvas'. The young man shook his head, showing them the palms of his hands, his eyes orbs of confusion. He pointed to his throat, opened his mouth and warbled something unintelligible. The couple asked more questions, determined to get any possible information so as to clear the air of the mystery. But the young man became frightened. He leaped off the bench, struggled through the tangling accusations of Matthew and Eva, and ran away as fast as he could. He was never seen again.

As the baby became more and more of a beast in the eyes of the community, there came a chilling realization among some people that the entire community was cursed with its arrival. There was talk that the baby was the work of the Devil himself, and that the members of the DeSilva family were agents of Satan. No one dared to look directly at any of the DeSilvas or even come close to their house. Someone started a petition to ban them from the community, but no one was willing to be the first to sign, and the petition was quickly disregarded.

One afternoon, Howard Ching was left to watch the store by himself. His wife Gerdy had run off to deliver home-baked pies to the church bazaar and had assured him of her return in fifteen minutes. She was already gone an hour when Marianne DeSilva entered the store to buy a can of corned beef. Howard Ching's jaw dropped. Gripping the armrests of his wheelchair, he suddenly lurched forward and stood staggering at the counter, shaking from head to toe, his eyes widened at the sight of the young mother of the beast. Marianne placed money on the worn rubber coin mat next to the cash register, but, frightened by the ghostly look on Howard's face, picked up the canned meat and left without her change. A returning Gerdy saw Marianne running off in the opposite direction. Worried, she went into the store and found her husband, tottering but standing, behind the counter.

"Howard!" exclaimed Gerdy. "You standing!"

Howard Ching thereupon collapsed to the floor. Her eyes filling with joyous tears, Gerdy fell upon him, praising the Lord while hugging her husband's legs.

"Dah . . . Devil . . . was . . . here . . ." he sputtered. Then he lapsed into unconsciousness.

Later that night while Howard Ching was resting, the phone lines of the community were buzzing about the miracle. In their small cottage behind the store, Gerdy was busy with an inundation of well-wishing, curious family and friends. When Howard woke in the darkness of the bedroom, his first thought was that he was dead and awaiting Judgment by a group of loud, drunken angels carousing in an adjacent hall. He realized that he wasn't dead when he recognized his wife's high-pitched voice describing the miracle. Howard slowly got up, rubbed his legs, then staggered across the room. He opened the door with hesitation, the bright light of the living room hurting his eyes. There was a sudden quiet. Everyone's eyes were on him. Then, clearing his throat, he said, "It was dah DeSilva girl. Dat bitch—she dah Devil!"

There was a noisy confusion among the people. Someone asked him for clarification. Howard repeated what he had said, then added, "Dis is dah Devil's work . . . making me walk again." Only his last four words were heard.

From that night on, with proof of the Lord's blessing and work in the restored legs of Howard Ching, there came a sudden change in the way the community looked at the DeSilvas.

The first day—a little over three months after the arrival of the baby—the DeSilva household was overwhelmed with a flood of phone calls, coming from nearly every other household in the community. After one bothersome stretch of answering thirteen calls in a fifteen-minute period, Gloria DeSilva yanked the phone cord from the wall. The following day came flowers and fruit baskets of every size and shape. And the next day pots of soup were delivered to the front door, each pot accompanied by a note of a similar kind to Marianne, stating in effect that the soup was made from a time-proven family recipe and was the best food for a nursing mother. Finally, on the fourth day, the community began paying their visits, though everyone was turned away by Gloria at the front door. She yelled at them, swore at them, yet they came back the following day, and the day after that—and the following days—always with apologetic smiles and roving eyes in the hope of getting a glimpse at what they now considered a holy child. Some of them desired to see the baby so badly that they tried to break into the house. But Gloria was waiting for them with her late husband's shotgun, and one barrel blast was enough to scatter them all back home.

It was about this time that loud arguments were heard almost constantly between Gloria and Marianne, though nothing was heard from the baby. In fact, no one had ever heard anything from the baby, not even a whimper. The only indications of the baby's presence in the house were the boxes of soiled disposable diapers left out for the garbage pickups.

One day someone remarked that she had not heard mother and daughter arguing for at least three days. Another added that there had not been any dirty diapers set out for the past two pickups. Everyone became alarmed. So early one evening a large group went to the house, which was lit brightly inside, and knocked on the door. They brought gifts again, from flowers to candy to pots of soup. No one answered the door, so they decided to force it open. But they found the door unlocked. Entering the house, they found no one in the living room or kitchen. Then, in one of the bedrooms, they found the lifeless body of Gloria DeSilva, stretched out on her bed. An empty prescription bottle was on the floor beside her. They searched the other rooms but could not find a trace of Marianne or the baby, though they found the baby's crib. The crib's mattress had been stripped of its sheets and was covered neatly with clean newspapers.

It wasn't until two days later that children playing by a nearby stream found what looked like the tail of a very large rat. It was wrapped in old, blood-soaked newspapers. Charley Nakahara brought it home to show to his parents, for it was unusually long and thick, but before opening the newspapers, which exuded a terribly strong smell, Josie screamed and ordered her son to take the bloody newspapers and whatever it was wrapped in them immediately out of the house. Charley dumped the newspapers in the rubbish can, and by the time the refuse workers finally came to pick up the garbage, the tail had decomposed badly; a pestilent smell was left lingering in the can. No matter how many times Charley's father scrubbed the can, the smell would not leave. The smell got worse and worse with every passing day. Finally, the Nakaharas were forced to get rid of the can since the neighbors had started complaining about the smell and how it was attracting swarms of flies from everywhere.

The TRIAL of GORO FUKUSHIMA

The afternoon Elizabeth O'Brien Lazarus was found dead on the bottom of Nakoko Gulch, her naked shot-ridden body bound with blood-soaked blankets, the members of St. Mark's parish were at the church, preparing for their annual Christmas program. Father Emile VanderHoeff was in the small airless room behind the chancel which he used as his office, where he was counting and recounting the thin offerings from the two morning Masses. The day when Mrs. Lazarus was murdered—she being the great-granddaughter of a Scottish whaler and trader who married a Hawaiian woman of royal blood and inherited all her land when she succumbed to the smallpox—was a Sunday, two days before the eve of Christ's birthday. The women were decorating the church walls with hibiscus and sweet ginger; the statue of Blessed Virgin Mary was draped with long garlands of plumeria and vanda and crown flowers. The men were behind the church, digging a huge imu in which the two hundred-pound sows that Frank Cambra had donated to the church and a dozen turkeys would be baked for a Christmas Day party.

A short while after a potluck dinner of Portuguese bean soup, baked sweet potatoes and corn bread, the choir took the stage and began practicing their Christmas hymns. The rest of the congregation gathered in the back pews of the church, listening and talking and laughing in soft, joyous tones, while the children went outside to play in the thickening darkness of the evening.

At five minutes to seven, a flurry of gallops was heard approaching the church. Charlie Vincente's ten-year-old son Harold ran into the church, followed by the other children. "Is Johnny Kealoha," he said breathlessly.

The luna, the foreman, from the Kanewai Plantation.

A small group gathered by the doorway. The horse had been tied to a kiawe tree and the luna had gone into the back door of the Father's study, the door through which the members of the church entered to give their confessions.

"Father! Please! Hele mai! Please come quick!" Johnny Kealoha was heard pleading through the thin wall that separated the back room from the church. "Dey get him now! Quick—befo' dey kill him!"

The choir stopped in the middle of a hallelujah, and a silence spread through the sacred air of the church. The Father cleared his throat and asked patiently in his thick European accent, "And who are they going to kill?"

"Dah Japanee boy," the luna answered quickly, "dah yard-boy—dah one work fo' Mr. Lazarus—Fukushima!"

"And vhat is he guilty of?"

The congregation seemed to hold its breath in anticipation of Johnny Kealoha's answer.

With a choke in his voice, the luna said, "He wen kill Mrs...."

The Father's clock chiming the seventh hour interrupted Johnny Kealoha. After the last chime, Father Emile calmly asked Johnny Kealoha for his walking cane.

With his face half-hidden by the night and the brim of his large padre's hat, Father Emile passed the front entrance of the church without saying a word to the congregation gathered at the door. Johnny Kealoha lit the way for the Father with a kerosene lantern. He unhitched his horse and followed alongside the Father down the dark dirt road toward the plantation. The lantern made a golden aura around the hobbling Father and Johnny Kealoha.

The congregation watched until the Father and the luna were only a small eye of light, then decided to dispatch a small party of the menfolk to look after the Father. Without lighting their own lanterns, using the luna's lantern as their beacon, they were far enough behind that the Father and Johnny Kealoha did not know they were being followed. As the menfolk approached the plantation with its syrupy pineapple smell undisturbed by a windless night, they saw a bright moving mass of lights under a large kukui tree. The Father slowed, but continued toward the lights. About fifty yards from the tree, the menfolk made out lanterns and about a dozen other men armed with an assortment of firearms. Hanging from one low limb was a dark, bundled figure.

The Father and Johnny Kealoha caught the attention of the armed men. The men from the church stopped outside the light of the other men's lanterns and watched in silence and in horror.

"It's done, Father," one of the men said with finality. "Justice has prevailed."

The Father said nothing. He looked for a long moment at the hanging corpse. He took his hat off and crossed himself. Johnny Kealoha took his hat off, too. Then Father Emile kissed his crucifix and began praying silently. One of the men lowered the body to the ground, then stepped back as the Father gave the dead man his last rites, even though Goro Fukushima was Buddhist. The armed men started down the road towards the plantation manager's house, leaving behind the two youngest of the lot, Mrs. Lazarus's younger brother, George O'Brien, and a plantation hand, a big Hawaiian boy by the name of Maka.

When the Father had finished the rites, George O'Brien and Maka dragged the body to a wagon and loaded it onto the bed. O'Brien asked the Father if he wanted a ride, but the Father waved off the offer. Then the two men drove the wagon into the darkness.

Father Emile and Johnny Kealoha stood motionless for a long while. Johnny Kealoha's horse neighed calmly. Then Johnny said something to the Father and they started to walk toward the plantation manager's house.

The men from the church meanwhile were left speechless,

and it wasn't until well after the luna's lantern had disappeared behind a bend in the road that someone had the sense to light his own lantern. The others followed suit, and slowly they began to file back to the church.

At the church, they told their wives what had happened, but only after they were outside the church again, having sent the children down the road home to the plantation camp. By daybreak, word of the incident had travelled wide and far to the other nearby camps.

Another story came on a Kona wind from one of the camps that Mrs. Lazarus was at least seven months pregnant when she was discovered by Espenio Concepcion and his daughter Ginny while they were checking on their frog traps at the bottom of the gulch.

There was little doubt in the minds of the congregation that the Japanese gardener, Goro Fukushima, had murdered the wife of the plantation manager. After all, if the Father said that Goro Fukushima had committed that sin, they reasoned, then God was surely the witness to the murder. And it had disturbed them greatly that Goro Fukushima had done such a terrible, unchristian act of violence right in the community. They cringed at the thought that behind Goro's always courteous smile a dark evil had been hidden. This was a shock for the congregation since for the past five months they thought they had begun to know him well; Goro had given up his Tuesday day off to maintain the grounds of the church, even though he was not a Christian.

He began work at the church soon after recovering from a serious illness; while he was incapacitated, members of the congregation, at Father Emile's request, brought Goro Fukushima baskets of fresh vegetables, eggs, and home-cooked meals. He lived alone, in a small room behind the company garage, his room once having been a stall for a horse. The people he worked for, the Lazarus family, did not treat him well. This was a known fact. It was in appreciation for the congregation's help that Goro gave up his days off to work at the church.

At the time of the hanging Johnny Kealoha could not

remember what night it was when he had gone into Mrs. Lazarus's warm, dark room. Straggling far behind the gang of men, their cigarette and cigar smoke lingering in the still air, Johnny Kealoha already felt an inexorable sense of guilt. He glanced fearfully at the Father, the Father's face craggy and white like the crumbling marble of an ancient gravestone; and he worried that perhaps the Father, being the direct connection to the omniscient Father Almighty, was listening in on his telling thoughts. Johnny nervously looked ahead at the swaying lantern of the wagon and said, "Father, what dey going do now, dah men, wit' dah Japanee boy body?"

The Father's face remained supremely stoic. Then he slowly shook his head, his lips pursed tightly as if to hold back a flood. Finally, he said, "Father, forgive them for they know not vhat they do."

The bedroom window was opened and Mrs. Lazarus was in front of her bureau mirror, combing her long brown hair. It was night. Johnny stopped at the window and he could see her clearly because the lamp, which was powered by the electricity that the Lazarus household had recently installed, was shining brightly.

Mrs. Lazarus was wearing nothing.

Warm sweat dampened Johnny's brow. He looked around worriedly. He stared into the darkness towards the front of the house. He was afraid that someone would see him waiting there, and he had to remind himself that Mr. Lazarus and Mrs. Lazarus's younger brother, O'Brien, had gone to Honolulu for a couple days to talk to a Bishop Street banker about a loan and that the lunas were all in Kanewai town at the Hookano home, carousing at a party for Harry Hookano's father's fiftieth birthday, where he himself was supposed to be going.

He looked back into the well-lit bedroom, watching Mrs. Lazarus comb out her luxuriously long hair, the hair falling from her brush like a silent dark waterfall.

Then she set the brush down and turned, facing the opened window. She looked out the window into the darkness where Johnny stood frozen and disturbingly aroused. And when Mrs. Lazarus smiled, it was like a siren beckoning, promising peace and unending passion.

Johnny's body trembled. He felt as if magma were surging and swelling throughout him.

The lamp light went off.

He climbed in through the window, the thin drapes brushing the tough hide of his neck.

Maria Texeira was sorting out the Lazaruses' dirty laundry and came upon an undergarment of Mrs. Lazarus that was stained with blood. "Oh! My Lord Jesus Christ and his Virgin Mother Mary!" she whispered, crossing herself. She then tossed the stained garment in pile of extra dirty clothes and muttered something derogatory about Mrs. Lazarus's racial background.

There was a soft knock on the back door. Maria Texeira curiously peeked out of the laundry room and saw Goro Fukushima at the back door, holding a large package that was almost as large as himself. Maria watched the Japanese yardman, remarking to herself how skinny he was but how strong to carry such a large box. Mrs. Lazarus answered the back door. Goro Fukushima tried to explain where the package was from with the three or four English words he knew but mostly with excited jerks and nods and shakes of his head.

"Yes, I know where it's from," Mrs. Lazarus said irritably.

Dah lady, she no look too good, Maria Texeira commented to herself as she regarded Mrs. Lazarus's rather haggard face. The manager's wife was wearing a light robe which did not cloak her swollen stomach. She get seven, maybe eight months already, Maria thought.

"Goro, bring the package in for me, would you? I'm not feeling too well."

She no look too good, Maria Texeira repeated to herself. Maybe I bring da lady some bean soup tomorrow. Then she decided against it. The Lazarus household ate very well, they had meat every day for dinner. Maria remembered the time when she was pregnant herself with her second daughter, how food was so scarce she was forced to chew on fish bones and eat wild dandelions to quell the deep hunger pangs. All the while she knew that the members of the boss's family were fattening themselves on beef and pork and throwing the leftovers to their pack of hunting dogs, scraps she could have used to feed her own family.

She gave a silent prayer to her Lord and Savior, in thanksgiving for looking over her family and keeping everyone healthy during those trying times. Then she began to think of her church and the preparations for the Christmas Mass and program, and this lifted her heart.

When Goro Fukushima came out of the house and passed by the laundry room, Maria whistled at him and waved a hand toward the laundry room.

"Where you get package?" she asked in a low voice.

Goro looked at her quizzically, smiling.

"Dah package." With a finger in the air, Maria Texeira drew an outline of the box, then pretended to carry it.

Goro's face lit up. He nodded his head. "Missus . . . babee," he said, making with his gestures an invisible spherical stomach over his own flat one, then patting it. "Pom-pom."

"Ahhh . . . you good fo' nothin', no can talk sense to you. Go . . . beat it." Maria waved Goro Fukushima off with a sneer on her face. Goro's smile dropped and he went off confused.

"Dumb Japanee," she muttered while sorting out the rest of the dirty laundry. "Dey no can understand nothin'." She loaded an armful of clothes into a basket. "Mo' bettah dey jus' work and no talk. No can talk to dem, damn stupidheads."

Father Emile got up on the morning of Christmas Eve in the gloom he had been waking to since his first visit to Mrs. Lazarus during the time of Goro Fukushima's sickness. Yawning loudly, as if trying to break a spell, he went to the outhouse, unbuckled his trousers and did his business. When he finished, cleaning himself with torn-off pages from an old Sears and Roebuck catalog, he washed his hands and went into the church for his morning prayers. After completing his prayers he crossed himself, looked up at the crucifix and was horrified to see the lifeless Japanese yardman instead of Christ. He clamped closed his eyes and prayed until blood seemed to squeeze through his pores. Then, trembling and worried that his confession had not gone to heaven, he reopened his eyes and saw that the evil vision had disappeared. He retreated to the kitchen where he rested from the ordeal, dabbing his moistened eyes, and brooded on his belief that the redemption was only temporary. Then he fried three eggs, which he ate with hardly a break for air.

The lunas had taken a break from the scorching sun, taking refuge under a large mango tree. "Mus' be dah devil in all dem Japanee," Manuel Rivera said. Across the field, the Japanese gangs were weeding between the rows of pineapples.

"No," Posey Lydell said. The part-Hawaiian sniffed the air made fragrant by the fallen mango blossoms. "Dey okay. Jus' dey no can talk wit' us."

"Dey work hard," Charlie Vincente said.

"But how can dah Japanee yardboy he can kill dah missus?" Manuel Rivera said, tipping back his paniolo hat and scratching his head. "Dah wahine twice his size."

"Dah buggah one man," Harry Hookano said. "Das right. Dah buggah one man."

"You really think he wen kill dah haole lady?" Charlie Vincente said.

"Dah Japanee yardboy . . . he all right," Johnny Kealoha said weakly.

"Is not what I think," Harry Hookano said to Charlie Vincente. "Is what ev'rybody think."

On Sunday, the day when Mrs. Lazarus was brutally murdered, Goro Fukushima was weeding the wild dandelions out of the flower beds in front of the house. He collected the weeds in neat piles; later, after his workday, he would go to the Japanese camp and give the dandelions to the wives to cook for their families. It was a hot and still morning, unusual for that time of the year.

Suddenly, at a little past ten, Goro heard a loud scream, followed by weak cries for help. It was Mrs. Lazarus and the cries were coming from inside the house. Goro straightened up nervously and, dropping the weeder, he rubbed his dirty hands on his pants, looked at the house, then towards the washroom, and again at the house. He was the only one around. It was Maria Texeira's day off, and the boss and his brother-in-law were gone for the day, having taken their horses and guns and dogs to hunt for pheasant up on the highlands. The cries for help persisted. Goro ran to the screened front door, hesitated, then braved the forbidden entrance of the manager's house.

Upstairs, he discovered Mrs. Lazarus moaning and naked in a bathtub half-filled with bloody water. He approached the lady of the house fearfully, yet wanted to aid her; she grabbed wildly for him and pulled him into her damp web of hair and arms. Then she went limp. Goro was barely able to hold up her slippery body to keep her from sinking under the water.

Downstairs, Josiah Lazarus had returned to pick up a tobacco pouch he had forgotten on the kitchen table. Going upstairs to check on his wife, he found Goro struggling to hold his wife. He was speechless. Seizing Goro by the collar, he threw the yardman across the room.

Mrs. Lazarus had opened her eyes. "Josh . . . oh, Josh . . . I'm so glad you're here . . ."

"What is the meaning of this, Elizabeth?"

"Oh, Josh . . . help me . . . it's . . ."

Lazarus caught her head before it could hit the back of the tub. He turned toward Goro, but the yardman had already taken off.

Goro ran breathlessly for two-and-a-half miles down the road to Kazuo Iwamoto's general store, and there he collapsed on the front steps, his mouth a froth of blood and saliva. Kazuo Iwamoto, his eyes bewildered and unblinking, helped Goro onto a cot at the back of the store. "What is wrong, Goro?" he asked in Japanese. He slapped Goro several times on the cheeks, but Goro had passed out.

When Goro woke up an hour later, he saw double—two Kazuos staring down at him. He covered his eyes, terrified by his nightmare of ogres. But when he heard the quiet voice of Kazuo speaking to him, he calmed. The first clear thought that came to him he summed up in one word: dandelions.

Kazuo Iwamoto stared at Goro in confusion. "What did you say?" he asked with a bad taste coming to his mouth.

"Dandelions," Goro said plaintively. He sat up at the edge of the cot. "I left the dandelions back at the boss's house. I was going to take them to the camp this evening."

Kazuo shook his head. "And that was the cause for your head to be beaten . . . because of some stupid clumps of dandelions?"

"No . . . no. That was not the reason why the boss did that."

"The boss did that? But why did he do that?"

"He was angry. He saw me with . . . with . . . with his wife."

"What do you mean?" Kazuo said, his eyes blossoming like chrysanthemums. His monocle fell from his face. "What did you just say?"

"No! I was just helping!" Goro cried. "I was helping his wife—she was very sick—there was blood everywhere—I was just helping her. That's all." He paused, holding his face between trembling hands, then added weakly, "She was taking a bath when something bad happened to her. I was just trying to help her."

"She was taking a bath? Something bad happened to her?" Shakily, Kazuo Iwamoto sat down on a wooden crate of dried fish. He sighed grievously. "You are very stupid," he said, shaking his head. "Do you know what they will do to you?"

"I was just helping . . ."

From outside came the sound of approaching horses. Kazuo silenced Goro, then went out to the front, his trembling hands clasped together behind his back. Mrs. Lazarus's younger brother and Big Maka were on horseback, each with a menacing shotgun.

"Have you seen Goro Fukushima?" O'Brien asked.

Kazuo shook his head stiffly. "No, me no sabe where him. Why you ask?"

"Never mind. If you see him, you tell us right away. Do you understand?"

Kazuo nodded his head. "Yes-yes. But why you like see him?"

O'Brien had a sickly pale look. "Never mind. And while you're here, gimme two bottles of your soda pop." He glanced about as if distraught, then dug into his pocket and took out two nickels which he flicked onto the store's landing. Kazuo picked up the nickels, went back into the store, swore under his breath at the white devil on horseback as he opened the bottles, and took the two sodas to the riders. Then the men left.

Kazuo pretended to straighten up the front of the store until the men disappeared from sight, then hurried to the back. He grabbed Goro by the shoulders and shook him hard.

"What did you do? Tell me now or I'll bring them back!"

Sobbing, Goro told Kazuo the rest of the story.

"It's not my fault," Goro cried. "I did not do anything wrong. I did no harm."

"They won't believe you." Devastated, Kazuo leaned back against the wall. But in a moment he straightened up. "Quick—you must get out of here. Forget your belongings. I will lend you money for a steamboat passage to Kaua'i. When you get to Kaua'i, you get yourself a job and send me back the money. But don't put your name on the envelope. Understand?"

Goro nodded. Kazuo went to the cash register and took twenty dollars and gave it to Goro, along with a new shirt and a loaf of bread.

"Leave now," Kazuo said. "If they find you here, they'll take me, too. Go into the bush and when it is dark, go to Honolulu and find the boat in the harbor. Understand?"

Goro nodded his head. Quickly he changed his shirt. Kazuo went out front, scanning the roadside, then signalled Goro to leave. Goro bowed and thanked Kazuo for an eternity, forcing Kazuo to shove him off with a brisk wind that had just coughed up from behind. Kazuo watched his friend run. Goro stopped for a moment to turn and bow again, then disappeared into the bush.

Kazuo shook his head. Then he looked in the direction the horsemen had gone, the wind now blowing grit into his face. Clenching his fists to temper the pain in his eyes, he muttered, in the tone of a bitter, masterless samurai, "Your mothers must have slept with pigs to make you!"

On the eve of the Savior's birth, Father Emile conducted a Mass that none of the congregation would ever forget; it would be the darkest hour the church would ever know.

There was already an uneasy atmosphere in the church. On the one hand, the congregation was anxious to usher in the joyous celebration of the Lord's birth; on the other hand, there was a bad feeling in the air, caused by the deaths of two people in the community.

That evening, as Father Emile lifted the chalice of the blood of Christ in front of the altar, he saw the eyes of Christ opening and blood gurgling from the mouth. The priest's eyes widened with fear; his body shook and the chalice slipped through his hands, bouncing on the floor with a loud dull clang. Father Emile tottered back, the consecrated wine having spilled over his vestments and shoes and onto the floor. There was a hush in the church as heavy as a dark cloud touching land but not raining, and when the altar boy, Hank Santos, finally broke out of his shock and jumped to the Father's aid, attempting to mop up the mess with his own clothes, the Father pushed him away forcefully. "Leave me alone, you filthy idiot!" he screamed in his native tongue. Then he stepped to Hank and slapped him hard on the side of the head.

(Twenty-five years later, while gossiping with her two sisters and three daughters at the home of her daughter-in-law, Mrs. Robinson Chun reminisced with asphyxiating clarity: "You know, I never seen one priest swear bad like that, 'specially in the House of the Lord. You know, I even saw Jesus's face crying on the cross.")

After the words had thundered out of his dry mouth and reverberated throughout the church, endlessly criss-crossing the suspended silence of the congregation and the sacred coral walls, Father Emile disappeared into the sacristy. There he took a wine bottle from a cabinet, wiped the chalice clean with the purifier, and filled it with the spirits. He then took a long swig from the bottle. Re-emerging from his self-confession and proceeding with the rest of the Communion as if nothing had happened, he uttered the bloodless Latin as if it were untainted by the blasphemous interruption of a few moments before, all to the increasing astonishment of an audience who had hardly taken a breath since the Father's outburst.

"De Father, de Son and de Holy Ghost . . ."

When he had finished giving the Communion, with the congregation still stunned at his outburst, Father Emile mounted the pulpit, opening the big book where his marker had been randomly placed two days before, and looked over his flock of mute sheep. In a voice little more than a whisper, he hissed, "Vhen de flesh is rebellious, you have to slap it down!"

"You know, I used to see dat Japanee boy go in and out dah missus house," Maria Texeira said to her friends in her voice of reliability. They were sitting under a mango tree at a picnic table on the church grounds. Some of the women were knitting, while the others were simply fanning the heat away from their sweating faces. It was a Sunday, and the women of the church usually gathered in the early afternoon.

"But you know what my husband said," said Constance Fung in an alarmed tone. "He tol' me only Mr. Lazarus get one gun li' dat. Mrs. Lazarus, she was all full of bullet holes." She shook her head while the other ladies gasped.

"No!"

"No!"

"Oh, my blessed Virgin Mother!"

"And dah boss, he no let nobody touch his guns except him or his brothah-in-law or his friends from downtown."

Obstinate Maria Texeira held her ground. "But I see dah Japanee boy go in and out dah house ev'ry day. I know. I work deah." She paused, letting the weight of her facts settle among the women. "And even dah Fathah would agree wit' me."

"Yeah, das right. Maria, she work ovah deah."

"Dah Japanee boy, no can trust him," Maria Texeira said. "I dunno why dey hire him. You cannot know what going on in his mind. You look at him, jus' like dah devil in his eye. Ho . . . scary sometimes when I think I used to work right next to him!" She shook away her exaggerated shivers.

"Oh, my blessed Virgin Mother!" Alice Kamaka cried. "Why dis kine gotta happen to us?"

"I know," Constance Fung said sadly. "Why, yeah, dis kine

thing gotta happen to us?"

Father Emile left the back room of the church, dressed in his flowing black robe and his padre's hat. He solemnly tipped his hat as he passed the ladies, then walked down the dirt road in the direction of the plantation, his bent frame making an awkward obtuse angle.

"I feel sorry fo' dah Father," Constance Fung said. "Been one month since all dis happened. But ev'ry day seem like he getting older and older. Jus' like he taking dah sole responsibility fo' all dis when happen."

"Why you say dat, Connie?" Maria Texeira said. "Das his duty, to see dat he know dah truth of dah matter. He dah link to Fathah Almighty. Das God's eyes and heart you see walking down dah road."

The ladies silently nodded their heads.

"I feel sorry fo' him, still yet," Constance Fung said. "He have to shoulder all dah responsibilities."

"Yeah," Alice Kamaka said. "And I heard he had to give dah last rites fo' Mrs. Lazarus body and dah Japanee boy. I dunno if I could do dat. And dah Japanee boy, he not even one Christian!"

"But he was one good man," Clara Vincente added weakly. Everyone stopped what they were doing and turned to stare at Clara Vincente, who made it a habit not to say anything more than five words at a time.

"Yeah, he was one good boy," Alice Kamaka said finally. "He come help us clean up dah church and dah yard ev'ry Tuesday. Was his day off, too."

"But we wen help him out," Maria Texeira said coldly. "Wen he was sick, we geev'd him food. At least he should be appreciate what we did fo' him."

"But he used to come ev'ry Tuesday," Alice Kamaka repeated.

Maria Texeira nodded her head grimly. "But sometimes I wonder if he was really dah devil. And you think he was walking around dis very ground we on right now!"

"But he was one good man," Clara Vincente said. "My boy and him was good friends."

"How come?" Maria Texeira asked suspiciously.

Clara Vincente continued with her knitting, not raising her eyes to meet the others'. "My Harold used to go fishing wit' him down dah stream once in awhile. Dey use to catch plenny o'opu and o'pae. Dah Japanee man, he was one nice man." Clara Vincente's eyes lifted steadily from her knitting and bored into the faces of the women, then homed in on Maria Texeira. Everyone looked away except for Maria Texeira, but finally she succumbed to Clara Vincente's admonishing look. "He nevah kill Mrs. Lazarus. He nevah touch her. I know dat fo' one fact."

Clara Vincente looked down the road at the diminishing, hobbling figure of Father Emile. "Even dah Father know dat," she said, going back to her knitting. "And he dah one who wen taste Mrs. Lazarus's blood."

Goro Fukushima ran through the bush in a fever, his soul burning from the angry eyes of Mrs. Lazarus's husband. The only other time he had seen such fire in someone's eyes was the time of the famine in his home province in Japan when his father had beat him for spilling rice in a puddle of mud. He thought of the boss's wife in her pain, in her agony. Was she in childbirth? Goro tripped over a dead branch and landed sprawling in a guava shrub. He crawled out, rested, and began thinking again about his hopeless predicament.

He was a foreigner in a strange land, his own people unwilling to shelter him. And he uncertain of where he was going. He did not know the direction of Honolulu. He had been there only once, the time he arrived by ship from Japan. The journey from Honolulu to Kanewai, he remembered, was very long and part of the way was over a long and winding trail which clung precariously to a cliff. How was he to find this road?

Then he thought of the Father, the white man at the church with that hairy face like an ogre's. Would the Father help him get to Honolulu? The Father was always kind to him; he would surely understand his predicament and help him get to Honolulu. The Father had always fed him after Goro finished the yardwork around the church.

He had nothing to lose.

He went back to the road, then ran as fast as he could.

A short while later he entered the breathless silence of the church, the first time he had ever entered from the front, and smelled the strange sweetness of flowers which were left in boxes by the congregation following the last Mass, and saw Jesus hanging from the wooden cross on the back wall of the chancel. It was a powerful and fearful sight, and with his eyes transfixed by the cross, Goro began to tremble.

The silence was broken by a cough from the backroom. Father Emile peered out through the doorway. "Can de Haus of de Lord be of help to someone?"

Goro presented himself.

"Yes, Goro, vhat iz it you vant? It iz not Tuesday yet, iz it? It iz a Sunday. But vhat has happened to you?" Father Emile regarded the dried blood on Goro's face.

"Pees hevlp me, fathah," Goro pleaded. "Pees hevlp."

"Vhat iz it you vant?" The Father's eyes narrowed as if to make his hearing keener. "Vhat iz it?"

Goro pointed anxiously in the direction of the plantation. He pointed at himself and then bowed and shook his head.

"Oh, I see," the Father said. "You have trouble vith your boss again. All right. I see vhat I can do." He rose from his bare desk, placing a marker in the book before closing it. "Come, my son. You and I . . . ve go see Mr. Lazarus."

Emphatically, Goro shook his head.

"Vhat iz it? Vhy you do not vant to go?"

Goro brought his hands together as if in prayer, his head bowed, his eyes pleading.

"All right . . . all right. I vill go myself. You may stay here until I come back." The Father patted a cot next to the desk. "You can rest here. I vill come back." Then he took his cane and hat and left the church.

Goro Fukushima was awakened roughly by Lazarus, O'Brien, and Big Maka. They lifted him from the cot and propped him against a wall.

Lazarus pushed his face down close to Goro's. "I'm going to teach you yellow dogs a good lesson for touching a white woman!"

"What you like us do wit' him?" Big Maka asked. "Take him down to dah Sheriff's?"

Lazarus shook his head. "No! Tie him up and make sure you gag him well."

The men gagged Goro with a towel and bound his wrists with heavy hemp robe. They walked him out of the church, heaved him onto a wagon, then drove to the plantation.

On the road they passed Father Emile, who had been to the plantation and now was returning to the church. He stared at the wagon and watched it pass. The men tipped their hats in deference to him.

They left Goro in the tool shed that adjoined the horse stable Two hours later, they returned with lanterns and a dozen other men. Johnny Kealoha was walking his horse when he heard the stormy mob and saw Goro being dragged out to the kukui tree. A noose was dangling from a low branch. He jumped on his horse and galloped away.

"Quick!" Lazarus said. "Com'n! Let's get this thing over and done with."

"Josh, I can't imagine how the hell this little Jap got hold of your rifle," Horace Tingle said, the son of the district magistrate. "I *do* know how carefully you guard your firearms."

"Never mind," Lazarus said. "The point is that he stole my shotgun and murdered my wife with it. Come on, let's get this thing going."

"Why, isn't this a scared little yeller sonavabitch!" remarked one of the men who had been recruited by Lazarus.

The men lifted a struggling and terrified Goro Fukushima to his feet, walked him to the wagon beneath the noose, then lifted him onto the bed. They lowered the noose over his head and tightened it around his neck.

"Take the gag off," ordered Lazarus. "Let him speak his last words to the world before God strikes."

Big Maka took off the gag. Tears rolled down Goro's cheeks,

but he said nothing. He cleared his throat, then spat on the wagon.

A swarm of termites suddenly flew in from the surrounding darkness and covered the men's lanterns. They fluttered around Goro, nearly covering his body. Everyone stood stone still in the momentary dimness, as if warned by a curse.

Lazarus finally called for their attention, his usual deep voice tenored as if someone had squeezed his testicles. With hands cold and trembling, he aimed the shotgun at the night sky and emptied the barrels.

A TOAST *to* ROSITA

When Rosita Kamali'i died of a Valium overdose, we went down secretly to his house to pay our respects. It was night, and we parked our bicycles in an empty lot across the street. We snuck into his front yard—the grass was growing wild and knee-high—and hid in the darkness under an old mango tree. The house was dark; we knew there was no one inside.

A flashing silent ambulance had taken his body away that afternoon. We and a few of the neighbors gathered along the concrete walkway fronting his house and watched as the paramedics carted him into the ambulance. One of the neighborhood kids, a friend of ours named Kimo, had found Rosita's body. He told us that he had been playing with his dog across the street when his dog suddenly stopped and began to sniff the air. The dog ran across the street and disappeared behind Rosita's house, all the while barking madly. Kimo chased after his dog and found the kitchen door wide open. There he saw Rosita lying motionless on the floor. Later, the paramedics found an empty prescription bottle next to the body. When the ambulance drove off and the people slowly walked back to their homes, gossiping among themselves, we decided to come back that evening to pay our final respects to Rosita.

Under the veil of a moonless night, Rosita's house did not seem any different than the other houses on the block. We could not see its high sloping roof, the intricate details of the huge recessed windows, the perfectly fitting moss rock that made up its solid foundation. In the day it was obvious that the house was not like any of the other homes. There was a breezy veranda with a beautifully stained balustrade and a front door made of koa wood. Above the spread of the mango tree, the house rose two stories, towering over the other houses.

    A while back, much of the land on the street belonged to Rosita's family. His mother came from an ali'i family; her grandfather had held some small but important position in Kalākaua's court. For her wedding gift, the old grandfather gave a parcel of land measuring approximately one city block. But the marriage was ill-fated. Her husband, a hapa haole named O'Connors, soon developed a drinking habit after impregnating his wife with the future Samuel Kamali'i O'Connors. He began to frequent the gambling dens of Chinatown, where, in a short time, he accrued an enormous debt. Section by section the property was sold off to pay the bills and gambling debts until all that was left was the property their house was on. Shortly after Samuel Kamali'i O'Connors's third birthday, his father was murdered in a drunken brawl with a rival craps player. Samuel Kamali'i O'Connors never got to know his father, and the only remembrances his mother had of him were of the arguments that stretched long into the night and the black eyes and bruises she had suffered from his hand. As an expression of her resentment for her late husband and of joy for her newfound freedom, she dropped the "O'Connors" from their names. She vowed never to marry again.

    But that wasn't the end of Samuel Kamali'i's name change. When he was in intermediate school—when we were still in diapers or just possibilities—he fell in with a wild and outcast crowd. He later crowned himself with another name: Rosita. It was this name that he went by from that time on.

II

    When families began moving into the neighborhood, there was an uncomfortable awareness that an ali'i house stood right among us. At first, our parents regarded the Kamali'i family as a sacred historical representative from our not-so-distant but cloudy past. But when Mrs. Kamali'i refused to come out of her house and associate with us, our parents began to despise them. As our father finally said, "Who dah hell dey t'ink dey are, t'inking dey bettah than us!" To compound things, one day our father saw Rosita with his long hair in a ponytail and his fingernails painted a bright red. Our parents forbade us to talk to the mahu and warned us never to go close to Rosita or else we'd go crazy and turn "funny kine."

Rosita's mother became sickly, and Rosita was forced to quit school to support her. Though they were from the ali'i, they did not have money, thanks to the late Mr. O'Connors. Finding a good job was hard; Rosita dropped out of school at the end of his junior year and had no job training or skills. But through a fragile family connection on his mother's side, he got a job working in the refuse department for the city government.

Word of his employment spread through the neighborhood grapevine before even his first working day. Some gave him a week to last at the job; others, not so optimistic, gave him one day. On the first day, Rosita came home beaten up. We were riding our bicycles up and down the street when one of us shouted that the mahu had gotten off the bus and was coming. We cruised down the street. With his shirt torn and blotched with dried blood, Rosita staggered up the sidewalk, his head stooped forward. We passed him, but he didn't seem to notice us. All he seemed concerned about was that he got home. We did not see him get off the bus for the next two days. But the following day we did. He was walking straighter, and we saw a shiner around his left eye. A few days later though, he came home with his white T-shirt in shreds and an ugly swelling closing his other eye.

We never knew what made him continue, but Rosita kept working. Whatever abuse he encountered among the rubbish men he weathered. He commanded a strange sort of respect from us, though we were afraid of ever coming close to him, he being a mahu and we thinking that perhaps we should continue to keep our distance.

III

As the months passed and Rosita stayed with his job, which was hard and physical, he began to build bulk on his lanky frame. His shoulders and arms began to puff up, and he developed the physique of a truly muscular man. He took to wearing tank tops and his well-defined, darkly tanned arms began to be a focus of admiration among us boys. We all wanted to grow up to be strong and to have large, powerful arms.

One day, while peddling our school fundraiser shortbread tickets, we went over to his house. We rapped the brass knocker a couple of times; our knocks seemed to amplify on the hard koa door. The moments were long and drawn out; we felt the hard thumpings of our hearts. Finally, the doorknob turned and the old koa door creaked open. All at once warm air rushed out, carrying with it the sour odor of a working man's body and the flowery scent of a woman's cheap perfume. Rosita stood before us. His large muscular arms bulged out of a bright red leotard top. A tight pair of gray gym shorts squeezed his hips. He wore his hair combed out, falling over his broad shoulders, and a red hibiscus was neatly tucked behind his ear.

"Yes, may I help you?" he asked in a deep but effeminate voice.

We stood speechless, fidgeting, until one of us had the courage to tell him that we were selling shortbread.

"Oh, I love shortbread!" he said. "Let me see. I'll take one from you, one from you, and one from you. There. Are you all happy now? How much do I owe you?"

One of us—God knows who—told him the price of a ticket.

"I'll be right back. Don't go away now."

He disappeared into the dark interior of the house, leaving the door wide open. We heard Hawaiian being spoken by an elderly woman.

"Never mind, mama," Rosita said from deep within the house. "Just the neighborhood kids selling their shortbread."

He returned shortly with a dollar bill and a lollipop for each of us. We thanked him and left. Down the street, under the shade of a large lichee tree, we sat, sucking on the sticky sweet lollipops and talking about our impressions of Rosita.

A few months later, we saw a police patrol car pull up in front of the Kamali'i house. A police officer got out and went to the front door. From our front yard we heard Rosita scream obscenities at the cop and the heavy door slam shut. We went out to the street and watched the cop amble back to the car, stop on the sidewalk to wipe his forehead with a handkerchief, then get back into the patrol car. He sat there for a long while; then, without warning, he started his car with a roar and left the street. We were curious what that was all about, but, since the incident was fleeting, we gave up trying to figure it out and jumped on our bikes, cruised down to the corner store and then went to the nearby park. When we came back an hour later, a big white ambulance was parked in front of the Kamali'i house. We rode up the street and parked in the empty lot. Two men in white uniforms were carrying out a long dark bag on a stretcher. Rosita ran after them.

"Leave my mother alone!" he cried. "Don't handle her like that! She has ali'i blood!"

He pulled on one attendant's arm. Two cops grabbed him from behind and wrestled him away from the stretcher.

"You pigs!" he screamed. "You pigs! Let me go! Get your filthy hands off me and my mama!"

The attendants quickly slipped the stretcher into the ambulance. They slammed the door shut and jumped into the front. Then they drove off.

Rosita collapsed on the curb, his head bent. He sobbed loudly, and his body shuddered. We stared at his huddled figure for a short while, then rode down the street and parked our bikes under the shade of the lichee tree.

"Dat Rosita . . . he real funny kine, yeah?"
"Yeah. First time I see one man cry."
"Yeah, one grown-up man."
"But he not one man."
"What you mean?"
"He not one man cuz . . . cuz . . . he one mahu."
"But he still one man."

"Nah, he not one man. He one mahu. Grown-up mans . . . no cry. But mahu, mo' like one girl."

"But he wen geev us candy, he buy dah shortbread."

Silence fell over us like the heaviness of the air and the clouds before a summer storm. We thought about the lollipops and the shortbread and the cops and the big white ambulance that took his mother away. We looked up the street where Rosita still sat, bent over on the curb and crying.

IV

After his mother's funeral, which most of the people of the neighborhood attended out of blind respect, Rosita began to drink heavily. He would come home from work and leave shortly after to his unknown drinking haunts. One Saturday morning, while we were bicycling past his house, we discovered him lying next to his mailbox. We circled back and stopped at the curb, curious and alarmed at his condition. Upon inspection, we heard him snoring loudly. A thin scum of puke covered the side of his face and had spilled onto the walkway.

A few months after his mother's death, Rosita came home with a boyfriend, a haole boy with a pot belly, flabby arms and a tiny face with rounded features like those of a menehune. Now, when Rosita went out—which was every Friday night—he went out with his newfound love. And they always called a cab. People on our street never called cabs; we thought that they were for the haole tourists in Waikiki or the better-off people of Honolulu. So when the cabs started coming up our street early every Friday night, we'd stop our bikes at the corner and watch Rosita and his haole boyfriend sashay down the steps and enter the taxi, usually absorbed in light banter, and we'd stare in fascination as they drove on by us to their destinations unknown.

Our parents were visibly disturbed about the two. It was funny how they talked about them without mentioning their names in front of us.

"Dey get no sense, dem guys," our father said through a mouthful of food.

"Specially when all dah others around." Mother looked at us hesitantly.

"Dey get no class. Why dey no go up dah mountains and do it, or go someplace else? People living ovah heah."

"Something gotta be done," mother said.

"Den you go ovah and you tell em."

Mother was silent for a moment. Then she said, "God giveth. He must have a good reason for it."

Father looked soberly at her. "God giveth, but he bettah take it back."

One Saturday afternoon some of the fathers gathered in our garage to talk story and get drunk. We hung around, outside of their circle, listening to them talk.

"Dose fricken mahus!" our father said. "Dey bettah get deah act together and get outta dis place."

"No joke," another father said. "I no like 'em around my kids."

"Dey bettah bag or I going break deah asses."

"Eh Mo," one of the other fathers said playfully in a strained feminine voice. "Maybe dey like you do dat."

The fathers broke out laughing. One of them dropped his can and beer spilled out, making a thick foamy circle.

"What dey mean wen dey say dey stay poking each other's 'okole?"

We sat under the shade of the lichee tree, trying to make sense of what the fathers had talked about.

"I t'ink dey mean dey going kick deah ass."

"Nah, das not what dey mean."

"Den what, den?"

"I t'ink dey mean dem guys going poke, like mommy and daddy do."

"How you know?"

"Cuz I wen spock mommy and daddy one time wen I wen inside deah room. Dey nevah see me, but."

A sudden, heavy rain from the valley began to fall. We huddled under the protective but leaky umbrella of the lichee tree. When we realized the rain was not about to let up for a while, we jumped on our bicycles and pedaled swiftly through the pelting rain towards home. The rain drenched us, but it was warm, and it made us feel clean all over.

Rosita's relationship with the haole boy lasted for another few months. One day we heard coming from his house yelling and screaming and pots and pans crashing. We heard Rosita yell, "Get the fuck out of this house, you fucking haole sponge!" The big koa door burst open, banging against the door stop, and the haole boy tripped out of the house, stumbling down the stairs. He quickly got up and, wiping his tears with the sleeve of his shirt, trundled barefooted up the street. Moments later, Rosita leaped out of the house, chasing after his boyfriend. He caught up with the haole boy at the corner and grabbed his arm. The haole boy shook Rosita's hand off.

"Thomas! I was just kidding!" Rosita pleaded. "I'm sorry. You not one sponge. I was just kidding."

Thomas turned to face Rosita, glaring into his eyes. Rosita began to speak softly; we could not hear what he was saying. With an adamant shake of his head, Thomas turned and walked away. Rosita flung his arms helplessly down at his sides, crying for Thomas to come back.

Thomas went a little ways and stopped. He turned sharply. "I hate you!" he shouted. "You're always telling me about your mother this, your mother that. You never told me how good I've been to you all this time."

"OK! OK! You have been good to me. Now come back."

There was a strained pause. Then Thomas turned and walked away again. Rosita stood at the corner, his thick muscular arms flexed and at right angles to his body, his hands opening and closing indecisively.

V

One day the mailman delivered to our house a long envelope with the state government's emblem on it. It brought with it a purgatory called progress. After reading it, our father ranted and raved, calling the government all kinds of obscene names and shaking the walls of the house with his powerful voice. We did not know what the letter said, and we were too afraid to ask our father. So we asked our mother.

"The letter," our mother said, "is going to take our land." There was a softness in her voice, a feeling of resignation but also of dignity. "Your father is angry cuz what little land we get, the state like take it to build one highway in the back of the house."

We brooded about the backyard that was a playground for us.

"Dey going cut down dah mango tree?"

"I think so," she said.

"Dey going cut down all dah buffalo grass?"

She nodded her head.

The destruction of our playground, our second home. We still could not conceptualize it too well: the thought of a freeway being built through our backyard was too abstract for us.

"Den what we going do?"

Our mother shook her head slowly. Her lips moved. We thought she was going to cry. "I dunno, boys," she said.

We went to bed that evening, thinking that there was something terrible and evil out there, making our father angry and our mother quiet and sad. Something was happening. It was like the feeling we all had when our father came home one afternoon, his eyes bloodshot, and told our mother that he had been laid off. We were not sure what had happened, but it brought a gloom over our family. Our father stayed home for weeks while the other fathers went on working; and it wasn't until our father went back to work that our house came back to normal.

The next day as our family was settling down for dinner, there was a loud knock on the door. Our father got up from the table and went to answer it. When we heard Rosita's voice, we snuck off our chairs and poked out our heads—totem-pole style—from the kitchen throughway. Rosita was doing most of the talking. Our father, with arms folded and leaning his thick body against the door jamb, nodded a few times. Though we heard the words "freeway," the "state," and "robbery" mentioned a few times, we did not understand what he was saying. After a few minutes he said goodbye and departed. We scurried back to our seats and waited impatiently for the details of the conversation. Our father sat down, cleared his throat, and began to dig into his dinner.

"What was dat all about?" our mother asked.

Our father continued to eat. He bit off a chunk of sweet potato. After a long silence punctuated by the chomping sounds of our father eating, he sucked his fingers clean and gave our mother the kind of look he would give us when we had done something wrong and nothing could stand between us and a good whipping.

"Dah mahu wants us to sign one petition," he said. "He . . . *it* wants us and the rest of the neighborhood to go against the government." He took a strip of dried fish and bit off a piece. "One good idea, but no can work. They too strong," he said between chews.

"At least somebody trying to do somet'ing about it," our mother said. Our father nodded noncommittally. "What you told dah mahu?"

"I told him I t'ink about it."

"I t'ink we should do somet'ing."

"I told him I t'ink about it."

"Mo. If we no do somet'ing about it, the state going run us ovah. You know that fo' one fact. If you not going, then I going sign the petition."

"I say I t'ink about it."

The next few days we saw Rosita canvassing up and down the street with a stack of petitions on a clipboard, talking with the neighbors, debating with them, asking them, persuading them, and sometimes begging them to sign. Early one evening he came back to our door. Our father got up to answer it, and we followed him. With a proud smile, Rosita presented us with a page and a half of signatures he had collected from the neighborhood. Our father sighed and said that he would put his name on the petition. Our mother, who had followed us, volunteered her signature. When she had finished, Rosita smiled and thanked our parents. He looked down at us; we were squeezed between the thick bodies of our parents.

"How about them?" Rosita asked, pointing to us. "They can sign, too. Dah mo' signatures, dah bettah."

"Dey only kids," our father said. "Dey dunno what is what."

"But if we tell them, maybe they can understand."

"But dis no concern dem," our father said.

"But yes it does. They live on this street. They one part of the community. Dey going be dah ones to suffah. What you kids have to say?" Rosita looked down at us, his dark eyes shining, waiting for a response. We fidgeted, averted our eyes from his, and partially hid behind our parents. Rosita looked back at our father. "They may be keikis now, but what going happen going affect dem later."

Our mother cleared her throat. "It's all right wit' me. They can sign if they like," she said. "I t'ink is important fo' them understand what is what." She looked down at us. "You kids like sign? You know what you signing?"

We looked at each other, and one of us blurted out that it had something to do with the freeway coming through the neighborhood and that was bad.

"See!" Rosita said jubilantly.

Our father smiled weakly. Our mother affectionately rubbed our heads. Rosita offered us the clipboard and plucked a pencil from his hair, which was tied back in a ponytail. We studied the petition, half-filled with names, our eyes wide with excitement; the fresh signatures of our parents were on the bottom of the list. Then, in turn, we grasped the pencil firmly and wrote down our names. When we finished, we looked proudly at our tiny markings, and it felt as though we had suddenly grown taller and stronger, that part of the world now rested on our shoulders. It was a powerful feeling.

The next few days we saw Rosita make his rounds to the rest of the neighborhood. Sometimes we heard bitter arguments, and sometimes we saw the neighbors nodding their heads approvingly. We asked the other kids if they had signed the petition, and to our surprise, they had not; they were never asked. We held that privilege like a secret honor; we let that feeling shine in us for a long time.

VI

Rosita organized a demonstration that was to be held one afternoon at the state Capitol. The night before, he had marched up and down the neighborhood, passing out flyers that announced the protest. We and some other neighborhood kids took stacks of leaflets and helped Rosita pass them out.

We decided to bike down to the Capitol right after school. During school, we constantly checked the classroom clock, wishing that the clock's movement would speed up or that there would be a sudden jump in time. After the last bell rang, we mounted our bicycles and cruised down the street, hopped over curbs, dodged slow-traveling cars, zipped through the narrow alleys of downtown, finally reaching our destination. We were excited, expecting the entire neighborhood to be there, marching along the perimeter of the Capitol plaza and armed with placards and slogans to demonstrate the power of the people. Instead, we saw Rosita, leaning against the statue of Father Damien, the leper priest, a pile of picket signs neatly stacked next to him. Across on the other side of the plaza, some haole tourists were posing for a group picture. We were off to the side of Rosita so he did not see us. We watched him for a minute or less; and then, reluctantly, we pedaled our bikes away from it all. We biked home in a silent procession, single file, quiet and perturbed, as the dark edges of the night slowly spread across a sky made red by the dull copper glow of the setting sun.

VII

We did not see Rosita for a week. We did not see him get off the bus from work, though at night we saw the lights of his house burn brightly.

One evening, as we came in from play, we heard our father swearing loudly. At first we were frightened, worried that perhaps one of us had done something wrong and that punishment was near.

"Dat fricken mahu!" our father yelled as he stood in front of the television.

Our mother came running from the kitchen, wiping her hands on a towel.

"What is it?" she asked. She noticed us gathered by the doorway. "Mo! Watch your language. The kids right here. What you yelling about?"

Our father said nothing, but stood fuming in front of the television, his large calloused hands propped insolently on his hips. Our mother came closer to the set, and we followed behind her. Though we could not understand what the newscaster was saying, there, on the screen, was Rosita. He was chained to the door handles of the legislative chambers, holding up a placard with the words, "Stop the Freeway—Now!"

"Dat fricken mahu. Dat crazy mahu."

"Mo! Will you stop swearing in front of the kids?!"

"Look how crazy he is. What he trying to prove, strapping himself to dah door? If he so concern about dis t'ing, why he no go do it dah right way?" Our father shook his head.

The camera panned to several uniformed cops who were arresting Rosita, making him unlock the chains. The next shot showed Rosita ducking his head into the back seat of a patrol car. There was a close-up of his face. We saw Rosita smile, and though the volume was low, we heard him say, "The 'aina belongs to the people. Stop the freeway!"

VIII

Later in the week we found out, through the neighborhood grapevine, that Rosita, as a result of his arrest, was fired from his job at the refuse yard. One afternoon we saw him get off the bus at the corner. He staggered up the street in a drunken stupor, his shirt ripped in shreds and dried blood all over it, and his eyes were puffy as if he had not slept for days. One night we were awakened by a loud wailing. At first, our minds still cloudy with sleep, we thought it was a cat. Then we heard a hollow shatter of glass. Rosita began swearing loudly. He swore and cried all the way up to his house, and when the heavy koa door slammed, we heard its echo reverberate up and down our quiet, sleeping street.

IX

So we went to the Kamali'i house to pay our last respects to our friend, Rosita. As a token of our friendship, we lifted a beer from our father and brought it along; wherever Rosita was, we did not want him to be thirsty. We liked Rosita; and though we didn't care too much about his being a mahu, watching his life and realizing that he had given a part of himself to us made us feel that he was one of our best friends.

That night we quietly crouched against the dark trunk of his mango tree. For a few minutes we studied the shadows of the house. Then one of us opened the beer and poured it over the tree's roots. A gentle breeze blew. We heard the creak of the koa door opening. Then the door slammed shut with a force that seemed to shake the house to its foundation. We catapulted across the yard, leaped over a low stone wall and raced down the street, all the while thinking that a cold hand of the unknown was ready to snatch us from behind.

The GIFT

It was the summer of 1962. It was the time around the Cuban missile crisis. I remember my parents watching that black/white/gray—a lot of gray—television and listening with a doomsday kind of attentiveness as President Kennedy went into the motions of that fateful blockade. I remember viewing on the television those secret maps taken by a U.S. spy plane of the Soviet bases in Cuba. It was a scary time, marked by the uncertainty that at any second the whole world would blow up. I remember that feeling very clearly. Everything seemed so gray, there was no good or evil, just that lousy feeling that something wasn't right and that the bottom of the world was about to fall out. A feeling of hopelessness. I was ten years old then, and I remember my parents watching the TV set in a glum silence, helpless, as if their lives were suddenly worthless and meaningless. It was a bad feeling that prevailed in our home.

A few days later, President Kennedy's gamble paid off, to everyone's relief. Nikita Khrushchev backed down and the whole world began breathing easily. But that helpless feeling did not leave my gut, I don't know exactly how to explain it, but it was like nothing seemed to matter anymore. The world around me—my home, family, the neighborhood, everything—seemed irrelevant. Nothing seemed to matter.

About a week after the Cuban crisis, when the whole country was resting but everyone was still nervous about the realness of nuclear war, we heard the rumor that our friend Chunky Kalama had died. Actually he wasn't really a friend of ours. (Our gang consisted of me, my cousin Davey who was a few months younger than me, and two other neighborhood kids, Willy and Georgie.) You see, Chunky Kalama was the neighborhood bully. He never used to fool around with me because we were the same height though he was heavier, but he used to push around most of the kids our age or younger because Chunky was super-strong for his age. Willy—whom Chunky also never used to bother because Willy was about Chunky's size, even though he was fat and couldn't scrap at all—told us a story once about Chunky beating up a kid two grades above. And Chunky used to hang around another neighborhood bully, Damien Mahoney, who was a year older than us.

Though he was much stronger than me, Chunky and I had kind of an "eye-balling" relationship; in other words, he kind of knew he could have taken me easily, but because I was just as tall as he was, he probably thought it wasn't necessary to physically lord it over me, he'd just give me the "third-degree" eye to keep me in my place. And anyway, I never made trouble with him to give him the excuse to beef with me because I was pretty afraid of him, though I tried not to show it.

It was my cousin who told me that Chunky had died. My cousin was just as skinny as me and shorter. And he used to get pushed around a lot by Chunky and Damien. It was night when I heard the news from my cousin. I was sleeping over his house that night, his house was just a few doors away from mine in a dead-end street, and he told me that he heard it from his mom that the night before Chunky had tried to get candy from the machine down at the service station after the station was closed, and when the machine jammed after he had dropped in his nickel, Chunky must have banged the machine and pulled on all of the knobs making the machine tilt forward, then fall on him, crushing him to death. I remember my cousin telling me this when we were in bed, with a thin blanket over us like a tent. He was holding one of those pencil flashlights, telling the story with his voice wavering and fearful. We couldn't sleep that night, or at least for a long time into the early morning hours because we weren't sure how to deal with this, a kid our age dying and he being the bully and not liking any of us, and we thinking that maybe his ghost might come back and search for us and haunt us in the dark of the night.

The next day we told the rest of our friends about what happened to Chunky and they, too, did not know what to make of it. We were sitting in the huge mango tree in the front of my cousin's house.

"You think Chunky going come back and make trouble wit' us or what?" Georgie asked, looking at me.

I shrugged my shoulders. "I dunno," I said. "He was mad at you?"

Georgie's eyes were wide and scared. "No," he said quickly. "I nevah do nothing to him. But he always picking on me." He looked up into the higher branches of the tree, then quickly corrected himself, thinking perhaps Chunky might be listening in and might not like what he had just heard. "Nah-nah, he nevah pick on me . . . dat much. Nah, he wasn't bad to me."

"What . . . you scared his ghost?" Willy said, then started laughing.

"Not. I not scared of ghost," Georgie protested.

"Not. You scared of his ghost," Willy said.

"Not! You scared his ghost!"

"Not! If I see his ghost, I whack him wit' my fist!"

But we all knew that Georgie was scared of Chunky's ghost. We were all afraid of his ghost, even big tough Willy.

Then a week later, a strange coincidence happened. Georgie's oldest sister died. He told us about her death when we were all in the mango tree again. He told us that his sister was sick for a long time, something inside of her that the doctors had said was "incurable," and that his parents and everyone else connected with his family had known that his oldest sister was going to die sometime soon. But he didn't know, he said, or wasn't supposed to know. He told us that his parents didn't want him to know about her condition, but that his sister had taken him to the side one day and told him there was something wrong with her. And we knew that Georgie liked his sister a lot, in fact, we all kind of liked her because she used to make these real ono-licious chocolate chip cookies for us once in a while and Georgie used to bring them up into the tree and we all used to eat up every crumb, they were so delicious. Georgie cried that day, up in the tree, and though we had often kidded Georgie for being a crybaby, we didn't that day because we knew Georgie was very sad and hurt. When he finished his silent crying on his branch of the tree, wiping his tears and hanabata on his t-shirt, we all told him how sorry we all were and then we started playing Superman and Batman and Georgie said he was going to be Flash Gordon and then I said that I was going to be the Blob from Outta Space.

We never liked Chunky and Damien, the big bullies of the neighborhood. And we should have been kind of glad that Chunky was not around. But something inside of us was telling us—I know that's how we all felt at the time, though we never told one another this feeling—that maybe it was all right when Chunky was around, even though he bullied us about, that it was okay for him to do so if that meant him not dying and still being alive. It was an awfully hard thing to think about: that someone we knew, someone our age, had died. We didn't quite understand what it meant to be dead. All we knew was that it was a horrible thing, that it meant that Chunky, or any other kid if that happened to him, would not be able to play in the park or climb the trees or hike up the side of the hill, or do anything for that matter anymore. Period. No presents to open. No birthdays. No friends to play with. No pets. No soda water to drink from the machine at the gas station. No fooling around with the pay phone at the station and getting two dimes to drop into the change return slot after tapping the dial tone five times, the two dimes we would buy two bottles of Diamond Head soda water with.

We were afraid of catching Chunky's misfortune, we didn't want to be the next kid to die, so we avoided the service station like we avoided Willy's house whenever his father was drunk and raving mad. Or especially how for a long time we avoided going near the empty lot near Georgie's house because that was where we saw that mad dog with saliva dripping from its mouth and Mr. Wong coming out of his house with a rifle and killing the crazy dog with two shots, and Mr. Wong telling us that we would catch something bad if we went near that spot where the dog had died. After a while, though, we cautiously went back to use the soda machine. That was the only place in our neighborhood where we could get sodas. But we never used the candy machine ever again.

It was a horrible summer for us. Watching the television watch the world was no fun. And two people we knew were dead. And we not able to understand any of this at all.

In the beginning of the summer, just before Chunky died, another family moved into our neighborhood. The Rezentes family. There was a father and a mother and three children, all girls. And Cynthia Rezentes was the youngest of the girls and very pretty.

I remember the day we first saw her. My cousin and Willy and I were walking down the street going to Georgie's house when we saw them moving in. That's when we caught a glimpse of Cynthia. She gave us a shy glance, then scurried inside the house. Willy was all jazzed up. He took out the short black comb he always carried in his back pocket, the comb he had swiped from his big brother, and began combing his hair, a big grin on his face.

We were ten years old then and entering the sixth grade in the fall; and yet, we all had that inkling for the opposite sex already, though we didn't know what we were supposed to do or why we felt that way. We just had that warm and tender feeling swelling inside of ourselves that felt embarrassing but good. We knew that when we got older we were supposed to be interested in girls; we'd watched Willy's older brother and Georgie's older brothers and my cousin's two older brothers go out with their girlfriends. Often we kidded each other about having a girlfriend, which each of us, in front of the other guys, would always deny ever thinking about or wishing, which of course was a lie.

In our eyes, Cindy Rezentes was very pretty. We all must have harbored a wish that one day she'd be a girlfriend; I know I did. And whenever we passed by her house, our hearts would start fluttering, we'd suddenly be quiet, or if we did say something our talk became nonsensical. And then Georgie one day in the mango tree broke out with a candid remark how he thought Cindy was pretty and that he wouldn't mind marrying her. We all jumped on that and kidded him until he almost cried but he didn't but he got really mad at us and left for home. We all knew that what Georgie said was what we all wished upon ourselves, though we never admitted that to each other, and that teasing Georgie was like teasing ourselves.

I remember those nights before falling asleep when my thoughts would wander to Chunky Kalama and Georgie's sister and about their deaths and about that disturbing gray feeling watching my parents watch the television and me watching the television, too, that gray Cuban missile crisis time. When my mind drifted to those dreary thoughts, I forced myself to think about Cindy and how pretty she was, and how, maybe, she would be my girlfriend and we'd be happy, holding hands and kissing like how Davey's brother did with his girlfriend. I'd think about that hot summer night when we were all in the mango tree and Georgie whispering that Davey's brother was coming with his girlfriend and we all became real quiet and watched them sit down below us and start making kissy-kissy and touchy-touchy.

Georgie came to my house early one morning with his eyes wide and excited. I was inside eating a bowl of cold cereal. Georgie came in and sat down with me at the kitchen table. He started helping himself to the dry cereal. Then he said, "Terry, try look what I found." He unfolded a soiled sheet of notepaper from his pants pocket.

I looked at it, spread out to the side of my bowl of cereal. It was a crude map of our neighborhood. I saw the square that was labeled "service sation" and the streets with their names. There were all kinds of neighborhood landmarks penciled in like the big mango trees and the fire hydrant and the empty lot where Mr. Wong shot and killed the mad dog. Then there was one house marked with an "x" in a square, labeled, "my house," and a dotted trail that led from "my house" down a couple of streets, then up another street to an old abandoned botanical garden. The garden had the name "Friendship Garden," which we could never understand since entering the garden was like entering a heiau or an old Hawaiian graveyard. At least that's what was told to us, we had never gone into the garden. Willy said that his older brother had seen an old woman with long white hair and no legs floating around up there. It was a story he often told us, which made us never want to go there.

"Whose map is dis?" I asked.

Georgie looked at me hesitantly for a moment, then said, "Ah—is dah kine—ah dah kine—ah—Chunky's map."

"Chunky's map?!"

I stared at Georgie with disbelief and horror. Chunky's map? The first thought that came to my mind was that the bad luck associated with Chunky had come to my house and was here to stay. Maybe I was the next to die. I was scared—very scared—and very angry at Georgie for bringing the map to my house.

"Why you bring dis map ovah here?" I said.

"No-no. Is not Chunky's map. He nevah draw dis map. Is dah kine Damien who wen draw 'em."

"Damien?"

"Yeah-yeah. Damien."

"Den why you tell me is Chunky's map den?"

"Cause get his treasure ovah here." Georgie pointed to the end of the dotted line on the top of the map, deep in what was marked off as "Friendship Garden," and at the end of the dotted line was a big red X with the word "tresure."

"Whas dis?" I asked. "Whose treasure dis?"

Georgie smiled uneasily. "Chunky's," he said.

"Chunky's?"

"Yeah."

"How you know?"

"Cause I heard Damien talking 'bout dah map. I was down by dah ocean wit' Willy and Davey, dah time you had to go store wit' yo' muddah and fathah, and den we heard somebody coming down dah trail and sounded like Damien and so we wen go hide in dah bushes and was Damien and somebody else, we nevah know who dah othah guy was. But dey nevah see us. But den dey was talking loud and we could hear cause dey thought nevah had nobody around but dey was saying Chunky wen hide all his ball bearings and his money his grandmuddah always geeving him, his birthday money li' dat, and he get dah map cause he wen draw 'em out cause befo' Chunky wen die he tol' Damien 'bout dah treasure he wen bury up Friendship Garden."

"So how you got 'em?" I asked, referring to the map.

Georgie smiled. "I dunno. I think Damien must've ride his bike down dah trail and wen he and his friend wen go, must've wen fly outta his pocket. Cause wen we came outta dah bush, we saw dah piece pepah on dah ground. Den I pick 'em up and was dah map."

I looked at the map again. Chunky's ball bearings and his money. He had the best ball bearing collection, two of which were probably mine. That I was almost certain of. I had them in school in my cubbyhole and after recess when I came back in, my ball bearings were gone. I wanted to go up to Chunky and demand them back, but I was too scared to confront him. And we all knew that Chunky's grandmother was rich, she owned a store or a bar or something in Kanewai town, and Chunky always had the best-looking bike and nice clothes and he always had money to buy candy and soda water at the service station. He always treated his friend, Damien.

"But . . . so what?" I said. "What we going do?"

Georgie looked at me with a kind of helpless look. "I dunno," he said. He looked at the map, turning it so he could see it straight. Then he looked up at me and smiled. "We can go find dah treasure and take 'em."

I knew he was going to say that, and my body turned cold in protest and in fear. "No . . . cannot," I said.

"Why?"

"Das . . . das . . . not our money . . . and ball bearings."

"You tol' me Chunky wen steal yo' ball bearings at school."

"Yeah . . . but . . . but . . . I . . ."

"Dah kine, Davey and Willy said if you go, dey go, too. If you like go fo' dah treasure."

"You wen talk to Davey and Willy already?" I said with a chill in my voice.

Georgie nodded his head.

And then, pulling out what I thought was the big stick, I

said, "But if we go deah and take dah treasure, den Chunky not going like dat and he going haunt us wit' his ghost."

A worried look surfaced on Georgie's face. "Yeah, you right, Terry," he said after a brief thought. "No can take dah treasure. Dah kine, Chunky's ghost . . . he going . . ."

Georgie didn't finish his sentence, but I knew what he was thinking about.

Later that morning in the mango tree, the others agreed with our decision. Surely, Chunky's ghost would come after us and scare us at nights and maybe even beat us up if we took his treasure. The question then came up of what we should do with the map. Willy suggested we give it back to Damien, but I protested, saying that Damien would then try to get even with us for taking his map. Georgie added that we all never liked him anyway so why give it back. My cousin Davey said we should destroy it then, burn it up so the ashes and smoke go back to Chunky. But Georgie disagreed, saying that it was too valuable, but that maybe we should give it to Chunky's mom and dad, that the map was rightfully theirs. And so we agreed on that, that seemed right. We decided to go to the Kalamas' house, which was somewhere behind all the kiawe trees across the main road from the service station. Chunky's family owned a lot of land on the down side of the neighborhood next to the ocean. Willy said that before his grandma died, she was a friend of Chunky's grandma and used to go visiting down there.

So, shakily—since we had never gone even a looking distance close to Chunky's house, we being afraid of his reputed big brothers whom he had bragged about once as being ten times his size and would back him up in any fight—we climbed down the tree and started down the street to the gas station.

We stopped at the station, as Willy said, "fo' one pit stop." My cousin went to the phone booth. We all looked around and when we were sure that nobody was watching, Davey tapped the phone five times and out clinked two dimes in the change return slot. Then he did it again and two more dimes dropped out. Then we went to the sodawater machine and bought our bottles of Diamond Head sodas; my favorite was orange, I never got any other flavor but that. And as we approached the candy machine we all cast uncomfortable glances at it, taking a sidestep away as we passed it, hoping that we were far enough away so we couldn't catch anything bad and unlucky connected with it.

"You think we going get Chunky's bad luck?" Georgie asked worriedly.

I shrugged my shoulders uneasily. I couldn't offer Georgie any assurance. I looked over at the other guys and they, too, had worried faces.

We sat on the corner of the gas station lot and drank our soda water while we looked across the main road at the kiawe trees and buffalo grass in the direction of Chunky's house. Then Georgie said that he had gone there once while helping his older brother deliver the afternoon paper, but the mailbox was out on the road and so he didn't get to see what the house looked like, but that there was a narrow road that went inside Chunky's lot from the mailbox and that there was a lot of haole koa covering everything. My cousin Davey took the longest to finish his soda, but none of us complained because actually we were all taking our time, not really wanting to push it and get going to Chunky's house. When he finally finished his soda, we warily crossed the main road, silently, as if we were entering an old Hawaiian heiau.

Behind the thick bush, we came upon sections of the land where tractors had cleared the kiawe. (Later, we learned that his family had sold a lot of the land.) We saw several homes coming up and heard hammers whacking nails.

We had followed the narrow winding dirt road for a ways in when suddenly an old black dog came out of the bush and started howling at us. We froze. Then Willy picked up a stone and threw it at the dog, and then I picked up a stone and threw it, and then we all started picking up stones and throwing them at the old dog. The old dog trotted away with its tail between its legs, hobbled away actually, one of its hind legs looked hurt. And then Georgie threw a perfect shot: the stone sailed through the tail and cracked the old dog in its hanging balls. The dog gave a big long howl and ran off into the bush. We laughed, we thought it was so funny. And then I told a story of the time me and Davey went to our Uncle's pig farm and threw stones at the pigs' balls, which were big and pink and low hanging, and we all had another good round of laughs.

Then, after we went a little further down the road, Willy snuck up from behind and grabbed my 'olo'olos, shouting, "Grab balls!" I jumped and yelped weakly. I then tried to grab his ones, but he was already running away with his hands cupped over them. So I turned to get the others, but Georgie and Davey had already taken off down the road away from reach. I turned back to Willy and shouted, "I get you, punk!" And he said, "Whop yo' jaws!" And I said, "Whop yo' jaws!" And then I picked up a stone and threw it at him, but he was too far away for me to hit. So I turned and started walking down the road with a sour look on my face, the two ahead of me taking side glances back to see if I was sneaking up on them, and behind Willy kept his distance. I was all mad inside at Willy and vowing to get revenge. Momentarily, we kind of forgot why we were walking down the road; unconsciously, our legs were taking us towards Chunky's.

Then Davey and Georgie stopped at the side of the road and gave Willy and me this funny, what-should-we-do kind of look. I realized that we were at Chunky's house. All grudges were immediately forgotten.

Georgie and Davey waited for us to catch up with them. We studied the rusty, flagless mailbox, then nervously scanned the narrow road that led into the property, haole koa bushes hedging thickly on the sides. Speechless, we looked at each other.

Finally, Willy said, "What we should do, Terry?"

"Why we no leave the map inside the mailbox?" Davey suggested, his voice wavering.

"Das not good," Georgie said. "Den my bruddah going find 'em wen he come down deliver pepah. Plus that, I hate my bruddah. He wen punch my arm last night fo' nothing. No ways, José, I going let my bruddah get the map and go fo' the treasure."

They looked at me for leadership; I usually made most of the important decision-making for the group. But this time I was hesitant to voice my opinion.

I don't know how the words came out of my mouth, but

finally I said, "We better take the map to his family cause das what we said we was going do." I guess I must have wanted to set a good example to the rest of the guys to show them that I was a good leader.

Then Willy said, "Com'n, Terry. You the leader. Go lead us in."

Inside, I kind of choked. But, without further hesitation, I started walking shakily towards Chunky's house.

We had gone a couple hundred feet down the dirt road, making a turn, when we heard a pack of dogs howling and barking wildly. We stopped in our tracks, listening nervously. Willy turned to me, worried and whispering, "Maybe is dah old dog wit' his friends." Then we heard a woman's voice shouting, "Kulikuli! Honey! Blackie! Shut up!" The dogs' barks and howls diminished to whimpers. The woman's voice gave us courage so we continued down the road.

We came to a flat grassy area. There was a line of coconut trees that separated the grassy area from the beach and ocean, and to the left of our view was Chunky's house. It was a small, squat house, it was dark in color, not brown or gray but somewhere in between. There was an old boat pulled up to the side of the house, leaning on its side, which a pack of old dogs and pups had seemingly taken as their home. The dogs came out of the boat and approached us cautiously, sniffing the air, then barking and howling again. The door of the house opened and an old Hawaiian woman came out on the porch, saying, "What I said, Honey? Blackie? Shut yo' mouths!"

And then the woman saw us, and she squinted her eyes with a confused look on her face. She said, "Yes? What you boys want?"

Nobody said anything; the others were waiting for me to say something. So I said, "Is dis Chunky Kalama's house?"

There was a long, very uncomfortably long pause from the woman, an almost sad pause, even the dogs stopped barking, or so it seemed. Just the coconut trees were rustling in the background. Then the woman said, "Yes, dis is Chunky's house." She looked at the ground, then at the dogs, then back at us and said softly, "You his friends?"

I was frozen, I didn't know how to answer that, but I began to nod my head. And the others did, too. Then I said, "We get something fo' him, something he—he—he forgot."

The woman motioned us to come forward. "Come . . . come heah," she said.

We approached her slowly, the dogs began to creep backwards, they began their barking again but with half the effort. The woman silenced them. When we came up to the wooden porch, the woman leaned on the railing and asked us in a kindly voice, "You folks like one soda water?"

Nobody said anything, nobody . . . but Willy. Willy said, "Yeah . . . I like."

"What kine flavors you folks like?" the woman asked, half turning to enter the door to get the soda.

We mentioned our favorites. The woman entered the house and returned shortly with the soda. She motioned us to sit on a picnic table that was to the side of the house. There she joined us with a cup of coffee and cigarettes.

"Which one of you boys is Davey?" she asked.

We were all surprised that she knew Davey's name. Davey said that that was he. Then the woman went down the list, asking who was who, mentioning all of our names, except Damien's.

The woman looked at us with smiling eyes as she smoked her cigarette. Then she said, "Chunky always used to talk about you folks, how you guys play so nicely together." Then: "Ohhh . . . my poor baby! Why dis had to happen?" And the woman began to cry, huge tears began dripping down her cheeks. We did not know what to do, we had never seen a grownup cry before. Then, as fast as she had started to cry, she stopped, wiping her eyes with the sleeve of her shirt. "I sorry I cry in front all of you. But I look at you folks, at yo' faces, and all I can t'ink of is my only grandson."

That made me start thinking: but I thought Chunky said he had big brothers who would back him up in a fight?

Then Chunky's grandmother started telling us—all stone-faced, speechless, not knowing what to do or think—that Chunky liked us all, that he often talked about us, his friends, giving him bamboocha marbles and shiny ball bearings. She told us that his father had died when he was a baby and that his mother worked downtown, how she and her husband, Chunky's grandfather, actually were raising him and were his father and mother, but now that Chunky's grandfather had died the year before and now that Chunky, too, was gone, there was nobody in the house but her.

She was silent for a long time. So were we. When we finished our soda water, we all told her thank you and she asked us if we wanted more sodas and Willy hesitated and was about to say yes, but I said no thank you and then the others said no thank you. Then she asked us to stay a little while more, and so we did, but just for a little while longer while she remained silent, smoking her cigarettes, and we silently watched her. Finally Georgie said he had to go back home, and so we got up and told her thank you again and began to leave. Chunky's grandmother, still sitting and lighting another cigarette, said to us, "You folks . . . you folks come back again. Okay?" And we nodded our heads and said we would come back, but we knew we would never come back.

It dawned on us after passing the sounds of the carpenters building the houses that we had forgotten to give his grandmother the treasure map.

Up on our high perch in the mango tree, we thought out loud about our visit to Chunky's grandmother's house and what she had told us.

"I thought Chunky had big bruddahs," Georgie said.

"Yeah," Davey said.

"Den how come dah grandmuddah said he was her only grandson den?" Willy said.

"Ah, Chunky must've wen lie to us," Davey said.

"Yeah," Georgie said.

"Yeah, he must've wen lie to us," Willy said, "and den he tell his grandmuddah how us guys his good friends." He paused, thinking, then said, "I wonder how come?"

"You know why, I bet," Georgie said, "is because he nevah had friends . . . Chunky."

"Damien," Davey corrected. "Damien his good friend."

"Yeah," Willy said. "Das right. Damien his good friend. But how come dah grandmuddah nevah say nothing 'bout him? And she knew all our names!"

Through all of their thinking-out-loud, I was silent, listening and trying to piece together everything. How did Chunky's grandmother know us when we weren't even his friends? I started wondering what was it that Chunky told his grandmother about us. Was it bad stuff? But the grandmother was happy to see us. If Chunky had told her bad stuff about us, then the grandmother wouldn't have been nice to us and given us soda water. What was it that Chunky told his grandmother about us?

Then I thought about Chunky, how he didn't have any father and his mother was never around, being raised by his grandparents, and how it must've been hard living like that and lonely all by himself, supposing that he didn't have any brothers and sisters. And then I thought how he wasn't really that popular around the neighborhood and at school, how Damien had other friends but he hung around Chunky maybe just to get candy and soda water from the gas station since Chunky always had money. I started feeling real sorry for Chunky, even though he used to push everybody around. Maybe he pushed everybody around because nobody wanted to be friends with him and maybe he wanted to be friends with everybody but nobody would give him a chance.

"Terry, what you think?" Willy asked.

I looked at him for a long time, still thinking about all of this, and I looked at the others and they were all silent, waiting for me to say something. And then I said, "We go get the treasure."

Everybody looked at me as if I was crazy. I knew they heard me and I knew they didn't like hearing what I said. I repeated myself.

Georgie said feebly, "But . . . but Chunky . . . das Chunky's stuff ovah there. Get his ghost going haunt us."

Willy kidded Georgie, saying, "What Georgie . . . you scared of ghost?" He laughed.

But I knew Willy was just as much against it as Georgie because his laugh wasn't convincing to me. And my cousin Davey was silent. He was turning a little pale, as if Chunky was down at the base of the tree, looking up, pounding the bark with his large hands, and threatening Davey never to come down or he'd pound his head into the ground, something that he had done at least twice.

"I not going fo' the treasure," Georgie said. "I not going."

"What . . . you scared?" Willy said. He laughed again.

"Not. I not scared," Georgie said.

"Den how come you no like go den?" Willy said.

"Not. I not scared. But I no like go."

"Ha! Ha! No lie. You scared."

"You scared, too!" Georgie said angrily.

"Not!" Willy protested.

"Yes-yes. I heard you say the time at your house that you scared Chunky's ghost come haunt you. I heard you. And you tol' me the othah day how you no like go down the gas station buy candy anymo' because Chunky's ghost."

"Not! I nevah said dat!"

"Terry, how come you like go get the treasure?" my cousin Davey asked, weakly.

I didn't have a reason. It had just popped into my mind that moment that Chunky wouldn't mind if we went and got his treasure. In fact, I was almost guarands-ball-barands sure that he would rather give us the treasure than give it to Damien. So I told the rest of the gang what I thought. Willy asked how did I know this, and I told him that I just had a feeling, especially after visiting with his grandmother. Willy now had a look on his face as if I had betrayed him. He probably thought I was at first joking about going up to Friendship Garden and getting Chunky's treasure, but now he knew I was serious, and since he had come off like he wasn't scared, he was jammed in a no-turning-back predicament.

Willy said, looking over at Davey for support, "Yeah, why you like go deah fo'? What you t'ink get?"

I shrugged my shoulders. I asked for the map from Georgie and he slowly got it out of his back pocket and passed it to me through Davey. I opened it up and looked at the map again, at the landmarks, in particular the one marked "my house." I noticed that the house was above the main road so it couldn't have been Chunky's house. And it was right on the street above the gas station so it couldn't have been Damien's house, since Damien's house was two streets away, near

Friendship Garden. And then I noticed the fire hydrant which was . . . that was the only one behind the gas station and . . . and . . . and . . . next to . . . my house.

I stared at the map in stunned silence. A creepy feeling came over me.

Willy said, "Whas the mattah, Terry? What the map say?"

I didn't know what to say. Or think. Willy moved over to my branch, and Davey and Georgie slid over next to me, and Willy took the map and started looking at it. And then I said, "You see the fire hydrant?" And Willy said, "Yeah." And I said, "Get only one, yeah? And das the one by my house, yeah?" And still Willy didn't catch on to what I was trying to say. So I told everybody what I saw in the map.

"Nah . . . how can be yo' house?" Willy said.

"You nevah draw the map," Georgie said. "I wen pick 'em up from wen drop from Damien's pocket."

"You sure das what the map say?" Davey said.

I took the map away from Willy and looked at it again. And I became more convinced of what I saw the first time. Why was my house in the map and why was it connected to the "tresure"? I couldn't think straight.

Georgie looked at the map and after studying it for a few moments said, "Yeah, look. Get the Ah Chew's mango tree ovah here. Look. And right next is the fire hydrant. And the fire hydrant right next to Terry's house." He pointed in the direction of my house. Then he looked at me and said, "What you t'ink Chunky wen hide in Friendship Garden?"

I told him that I didn't know, but that I had a hunch he had hid money and his ball bearing collection. Then I asked him if he was still sure that Damien had drawn the map and not Chunky. Georgie said, "Yeah." And then added, "I dunno."

I was trying to figure out why Chunky had connected my house with the treasure, if he had drawn the map, when Davey said bravely, "Com'n. Les go find dah treasure."

We looked at each other with faces doubtful but with a touch of adventure. Then we shrugged our shoulders and climbed down the mango tree and started off towards Friendship Garden.

We passed Cindy Rezentes's house and her dogs greeted us with angry barks. We looked towards her house and heard the strains of a Frankie Avalon song. But we walked on without thinking much about her, our minds were heavy with more important matters.

Willy looked at the map. "Dah stuff suppose to be buried by one fishpond."

"Where?" Georgie said, looking at the map. "No mo' one fishpond in Friendship Garden."

"How you know?" I asked Willy.

"Cause it say 'fishpond' on the map," Willy said. "Must be buried right ovah there."

"What fishpond?" Davey said.

"How you know no mo' one fishpond?" Willy asked Georgie.

"Cause, my bruddah said only get trees and rocks up there."

"But he nevah say had one fishpond or not, eh, ovah there?" Davey said.

"No," Georgie said.

"But no mo' fishponds up in the mountains," I said.

"Where it say get one fishpond?" Georgie asked. "Where?"

"It say right heah," Willy said emphatically, pointing to a word on the map in the area designated as Friendship Garden.

Georgie looked at the map. Then he started laughing. "Dat no say 'fishpond,'" he said. "Stay read 'Friendship'!"

We all started laughing up. Willy became irritated.

"How you know get treasure up deah?" Willy asked Georgie sourly.

"Das what the map said," Georgie said.

"But how you know? You dunno."

"I know," Georgie said. "You watch. I betchu all yo' marbles get treasure buried up there."

"Not."

"Yes-yes."

"Den how you know the treasure stay buried?" Willy said.

"Gotta be," Georgie said. "Treasures, dey always stay buried."

"Maybe dah stuff stay in one box and just on dah ground,"

Willy said. "You dunno."

"No," I said to Willy. "But you dunno, too."

"Dah stuff stay buried," Davey said. "I know."

"How you know?" I asked.

"I jus' know," Davey said. "Chunky, he would do something like dat. Bury his treasure so nobody find 'em."

We started up a road that climbed a hill; at the top of the road was Friendship Garden. But before getting there, we had to pass Damien's house.

"When we get ovah there," I said, referring to Damien's house, "we bettah be quiet, or else Damien going spock us and try make trouble."

The others nodded their heads.

As we cautiously approached Damien's house, we heard a loud scream, like that of a girl frightened by a big fat toad. We heard a deep voice yelling, "I tol' you no fuck wit' my things!"

"I said I sorry!"

There was another scream, followed by a loud slap.

"I going tell Mommy!"

We realized it was Damien screaming and crying; the other voice was that of his older brother.

"Go—punk! Tell Mommy! And I going bus' yo' ass again! Go! Tell Mommy!"

Damien was crying loudly, then he screamed again; in our minds we saw Damien's older brother raising a big hand.

"No! No! I sorry! I not going tell Mommy! No hit me, Bobby! No hit me! I sorry! I not going play wit' yo' stuff!"

"You fucking punk. I catch you fucking wit' my things one mo' time, I going geev you one 'nother dirty licking. You heard?"

There was a pause. Meanwhile, unconsciously, we had slowed down to a snail's pace, our ears listening intently to what was happening. We had never heard Damien—or Chunky, for that matter—crying like a girl. They were the bullies and you never heard or saw those kinds of things. So it was a very sobering experience for us to hear Damien cry and get beaten up by his older brother.

"You heard—you punk? I cannot hear you!"

"Yeah, Bobby."

"I cannot hear!"

"YEAH, BOBBY!"

"All right den. Beat it! Scram! Out! Now!"

We heard a door open and shut. We realized we were stopped in front of Damien's house, so quickly we scurried on, afraid to have Damien see us and realize that we had heard everything that went on.

We continued on to the end of the road where Friendship Garden began. Nailed to a tree was a sagging sign, which read "Enter At Your Own Risk." Giant trees flanked the entrance, which had stone steps climbing in, and inside the Garden was dark and quiet. It was spooky.

We looked at each other blankly, not knowing what to do next. Then Georgie took out the map and looked at it. "Get one bridge inside we gotta go across. Den one 'swinging banyan tree.' Den dah treasure going be by one Japanee church."

"One what? What you talking 'bout?" I said.

"One Japanee church?" Davey said.

"Yeah, das what it say," Georgie said.

I took the map from him and studied it. One swinging banyan tree, before that one bridge to cross, then one Japanee church. That was what was written. And drawn in.

We looked into the Garden again. And for a moment, I wished I hadn't made that suggestion of going after the treasure.

No one was making a move, so I said, "Come on. We going or what?"

No one said anything. I didn't want to lead the group in. I was hoping one of them would refuse to go in, or suggest we leave. But none of them said anything. I was left standing not knowing what to do, the others watching me from the corners of their eyes for my first move. They were ready to go in, but they wanted me to lead them.

Then Davey said, "Les go in." And suddenly he took the lead and started in. And then Willy followed, and before I could make out what was going on, Georgie was in and I was at the back of the line, feeling a bit disappointed that they did not wait for me to be the leader.

Swarms of mosquitoes attacked us. We found ourselves ducking our heads under low-hanging vines and climbing a narrow trail that was covered with rotting leaves and followed alongside a dried up stream. Parts of the trail had crumbled down to the stream, and we had to jump over those broken sections or swing across using the low hanging vines as handles. Then the trail flattened for a while, and we entered a grove of bamboo. We tried to break off some of the bamboo at the base to take home and use as fishing poles, but they were too green and too tough to break. We finally gave up, making a note to ourselves that if we came up here a next time we'd bring a knife to cut the bamboo.

The trail started to climb again. We passed tall paperbark trees; we tore off their flaking skins and tossed them around. Then, we started wondering: where is this bridge we are supposed to cross?

Willy looked at the map. "Says right heah," he said, pointing to the bridge. "Dah bridge. And get one stream running underneath. Look."

"Yeah, one stream," I said.

We looked around; we had left the dried-up stream behind.

"But where dah bridge?" Georgie said. "You t'ink we wen go dah wrong way or what?"

I shrugged my shoulders.

Davey took the map, saying, "Maybe . . . "

A wind blew into the Garden and we heard a chorus of moans coming from all around us. The sounds were probably branches rubbing against each other and leaves rustling, but to us, the sounds were frightening. We looked around, our eyes widening, thinking we were in the midst of ghosts; perhaps Chunky's ghost was about to pounce on us. I remember thinking about the story Willy told us about that old woman with no legs, floating around Friendship Garden. I became petrified; I remember telling myself that I was not going to say what I was thinking to the others. But looking at them, I had a funny feeling that they were thinking the same thing that I was thinking.

Then Willy did a bold thing. He picked up a stone and threw it deep into the bush. We heard it thrash through the trees. Then a thought flashed through my mind; I remembered my grandmother once telling me and my sister that if ever you come across a spirit and the spirit is making you real scared, the best thing to do is to make the spirit think you're not afraid of it. And so I picked up a stone, too, and threw it with all my might in the direction Willy threw his. And I yelled with the release of the stone. Willy picked up another and threw it. I picked up another and we both smiled boldly at the others and then they caught on and soon we were barraging the area with all the stones we could find or dig up with our fingers and nails, and even throwing broken branches and anything else that was on the ground.

We started laughing. Suddenly, we were the army fighting the invasion of the Martians, and we were winning. Georgie took a stick he found lying around and that became his rifle. Now the stones were hand grenades, and the wind sounds of the Garden were overwhelmed by our shrills and simulated explosions. Then Davey found something that started us back on track.

There was a concrete block that he had discovered while picking up a stone next to it. The block was covered with moss and mud and it was partially sunk at an angle into the ground. But it was squarish and had a flat surface, which were the reasons it caught his attention. He called us over. Georgie wiped his hands over the flat surface, clearing away the rotten leaves and dirt, uncovering an inscription. It read: 1937.

"What dis mean?" Willy said.

"I dunno," Davey said.

"Mus' be from one building or something," I said. "Dah old kine buildings, dey get dah old kine dates stuck on 'em."

"What building get up heah?" Georgie said with disbelief.

"I dunno," I said. "Maybe had one building up heah and dey wen tear 'em down."

"Who wen tear 'em down?" Georgie said.

I shrugged my shoulders.

"Maybe was something else," Davey suggested.

"Yeah, maybe was something else," Willy said.

"What?" Georgie asked.

"I dunno," Davey said. "But something else."

"1937 . . ." Willy murmured. "Wow . . . das real old."

"Yeah," Davey said.

"Dis Garden must be at least dat old," I said.

"Yeah," Willy said.

And then Davey made another of his remarkable discoveries. Looking down to the side of the trail, he saw what were once the low concrete-formed railings of the bridge. "Eh! Dis is dah bridge we standing on right now!" he said.

Sure enough, after brushing off some of the debris area we were standing on, we discovered a concrete slab. And we found a small tunnel underneath that had permitted the waters of a now nonexistent stream to flow through.

"Dah bridge!" we yelled.

Georgie took out the map and we all looked at it. The bridge, then right after it the swinging banyan tree. Then . . . the Japanee church?

We continued on the trail. The trail climbed and took a turn, and right after the turn there stood a huge banyan tree with vines hanging down everywhere under its huge top. It loomed up on the side of a hill, silent and still, looking like a gigantic dark jellyfish-kind of monster. We didn't care to test the long straggly vines and play Tarzan; we passed the banyan tree quickly. If the tree had been in a less hostile environment, we would've run up to the tree and swung on the vines.

Then the trail started descending, it was covered with needles from shaggy ironwood trees and there was a mint-like scent in the air, probably from the guava bushes scattered about. We came upon a broken bird bath and further down the trail we found a miniature pagoda, made out of concrete.

"Das dah Japanee church!" Georgie exclaimed.

"Yeah, man!" Davey said.

We surrounded the pagoda. It was set on a square concrete slab, covered with bird shit and dark green moss and was as tall as me.

Davey said, "So where the treasure?"

Georgie looked at the map. "The map say suppose to be here. Look. The 'x' mark right next to dah Japanee church. Look."

The 'x' mark was to the left of the pagoda. We looked there, but all we found were a rotten guava, pine cones and a lot of pine needles. No treasure.

"You sure you no have the map upside down?" Willy said.

"Go look den," Georgie said.

"Das what the map says," I added.

We looked to the right of the pagoda, behind it, in front of it. We raked up the rubbish on the ground and gathered it all in one pile. We dug shallow holes with pointed sticks into the ground. Then we sifted through the rubbish. Still, nothing.

"I t'ink Chunky playing one big joke on us," Willy finally said. We were sitting around the pagoda, slapping away the mosquitoes.

"Yeah, I t'ink so," I said.

"But wasn't one joke on us," Georgie said, "was suppose to be fo' Damien cause was Damien's map."

We agreed.

"But we dah ones getting one kick in dah 'okole," Willy said. "Was yo' fault, Georgie. You dah one wen show us dah map."

"Eh, I nevah know," Georgie said bitterly.

"Yeah, was yo' fault," I said.

"Eh, I nevah tell you folks go find the treasure," Georgie said defensively. "Was you guys fault believe in the map."

Davey got up and looked at the pagoda. Then he kneeled and squeezed his hand into a narrow opening. He brought his hand out clutching a wad of wet paper.

"Whas that?" I asked.

"Huh?" Georgie said.

"That . . . what you got, Davey?" I asked.

We got up. Davey began carefully opening up the folded piece of paper, wet from the rain and a bit muddy. The folds of the paper broke apart. There was something written on the paper, we could see that ink was diffused in the paper by the moisture. Davey laid out the bits of paper on the ground, fitting the pieces together, and though the ink was blurred, we still could make out the words. The message read: "Whop yor jaws Damien."

"You see! Was one big joke!" Willy said, proud that he had stated his premonition before this.

"You see, wasn't me," Georgie said. "Dis was suppose to be fo' Damien."

But I was disappointed. We were all disappointed. We looked silently at the bits of paper that Chunky had written to his "good" friend, Damien. We looked around at the trees and bush, which were still and quiet, as if listening to our thoughts. Willy suggested we leave. We left the note on the ground. Georgie folded the map and put it back in his pocket. Single file, this time with me leading the pack, we went down the trail, our ears sensitive to the listening trees and to the silence and to an occasional leaf-rustling wind, but not as afraid as when we first came up.

We saw Damien sitting in the front yard of his house, throwing small stones into the road. He saw us coming and stopped throwing for a moment, then started again. When we came near enough to hear, he said sarcastically, "What you guys looking at?"

I told myself that I was looking at one big fat crybaby. But I didn't dare say that.

Damien started throwing stones at our feet. We continued walking, giving him stink eye, but making sure we didn't stare at him too long. He kept on throwing the stones at us. He started laughing at us. He threw a stone that struck Davey's head squarely. That's when Davey stopped, turned around, and shouted at Damien with the angriest words I ever heard him say. Right then and there, I thought my ass was grass.

"You sucken Damien!" Davey shouted. "You bettah quit that, or we going broke yo' head!"

Damien, stunned at Davey's sudden, unexpected outburst, got up, throwing down a handful of small stones. "What you said, you punk?" he said, with a terrible mad streak in his eyes.

"You heard what I said," Davey said. "Punk."

Damien ran to us. My legs suddenly turned like jelly; if I tried to run, my legs wouldn't have carried me. Terrified, I looked at Willy and Georgie and they, too, were scared. I saw Willy looking at Damien's house for Damien's brother, or brothers, to pile out and attack us with their big knuckles. I felt very small that moment, Willy and Georgie looked very small, too. Damien came up to Davey and said, "What you said, punk?" Davey's legs were shaking, and before he could answer, Damien gave him a tremendous shove and Davey flew backwards and landed on his elbows and 'okole on the asphalt. "What you called me, you punk Davey?"

Davey was near to crying, his eyes were moistening. Damien lorded it over him like the bully he was, he feigned a kick at Davey, making Davey wince with this helpless look on his face and shield himself with a scraped arm.

Then, something came over me, Georgie, and Willy. I can't explain what exactly it was. It might have been because our friend (my friend and cousin) needed help; he looked so desperately weak fallen on the ground, ready to accept one of the many beatings we suffered as a group. Or perhaps it was the anger and disappointment of finding no treasure, having to go into a dangerous and spooky place like Friendship Garden on a wild goose chase. Or maybe it was knowing that Chunky was not around to back Damien up. And maybe it was also because we had read that note and somehow realized that Chunky and Damien were never that tight as friends, they had a common denominator, being bullies, but that was it. And maybe it was also because we saw the other side of Damien, the crybaby, something we thought we'd never see. Or maybe it was because we were sick and tired of being picked on again.

Maybe it was all the reasons above.

But whatever the reason, or reasons, Georgie and Willy and me all at once pounced on Damien, punching him and pushing him and knocking him to the ground. My fist connected on his mouth and I felt the bite of his teeth and the warmth of his saliva. He started to bleed from the mouth, though I don't think it was my fist that did it because I didn't punch him that hard; in his surprise, he must have bit himself on the lip or tongue. But the blood was pouring from his mouth and suddenly we all felt like victors. For a long moment, Damien was on the ground, looking up at us with the eyes of a scaredy-cat. Davey got up and came between us and started yelling at him that he'd better watch out or we'll bust his ass some more. Damien got up fast and shakily, retreating to his yard. He turned and started yelling at us, "You bettah watch out or I going call my bruddah come beat you guys up!"

Davey shouted, "Whop yo' jaws, Damien!"

We started yelling at him in unison while holding our jaws, "Whop yo' jaws, Damien! Whop yo' jaws! Whop yo' jaws!" We laughed. Then, from inside the house, came the deep voice yelling at Damien. "Damien! Get yo' ass in the house!"

We continued down the street, mimicking Damien's frail remark, laughing in pure abandonment, repeating our rallying cry over and over again, loudly, getting so wrapped up in our celebration that the driver in the car behind us had to wail his horn for a long burst before we realized we were blocking his path.

A couple of weeks later we started school again. But what started as a dreary, empty-feeling summer, ended on a nice high note for us. Damien never bossed us around again. He was a grade above us so we never saw him much in school anyway, and even around the neighborhood he never came around our territory anymore.

It wasn't until school was in its fourth or fifth month and in the beginning of the rainy winter season when we went back to Chunky's house. We thought we would never go back there, but we did because—though long months had passed—we harbored a guilty feeling that we had something of Chunky's that rightfully belonged to his grandmother. So we went down to the house—me, Georgie and Willy. (Davey had caught a cold from school and hadn't gone to class for a week.) And Georgie brought that piece of paper of a map.

The road was full of muddy potholes and we played a game of going between them and jumping over the biggest ones. Willy fell in one and soaked his pants in the yellowish clay mud. But we were all muddy anyway so that didn't really matter. When we got close to the house we became cautious for the dogs, but the dogs weren't barking, even when we got to the front steps of the house. In fact, we didn't see one dog there. The house looked deserted. We knocked on the door and waited. There was no answer. We knocked again, then decided to leave the map on the front steps and go.

Just as we were a dozen steps away from the front porch, the door opened and we heard the voice of Chunky's grandmother. "Chunky? Is you?" she said. Her voice was old and withered and thin and breaking. She squinted her eyes. Her hair was all white; she had gotten very old in the short time since we last saw her. She was almost unrecognizable. "Who's dat? Rose?"

"No," I said. "We . . . we . . . Chunky's friends."

She looked in our direction with a perturbed look. Then a dry weak smile came to her face. "Oh . . . you Chunky's friends. Yeah-yeah. Come heah." She waved us to come.

We moved slowly, confused about what she had said.

"Wait right heah," she said to us when we got to the bottom of the porch steps. She disappeared inside for a moment or two, then reappeared with a small cardboard box. She offered the box to us. Georgie went up the steps and took it from her. She said, "Chunky tell me geev dis box to you folks. He say he not going use 'em anymo.'"

We thanked her without looking what was inside it. Then she closed the door without saying another word.

We left. We decided to open the box, which was heavy and all taped up, at my house since my house was the closest and we didn't want to open it up down there because of the mud. When we opened the box we found a note and the box filled with ball bearings—two of which I knew were mine—and many beautiful glass marbles. We looked further in the box and found ten dollars and a thick stack of baseball cards and five complete Martian card collections. There were a few comic books on the bottom of the box, too.

Then we unfolded the note and read it, and even till today, I don't know what it meant or why it was there. The note read: "Sorry."

An OLD FRIEND

Camilla told me about the hot spring of water that had suddenly broke through the rocky ground behind our duplex, on the neighbor's side of the yard. The backyard was narrow and covered with small lava rock, and, beyond it, the grassy land sloped gradually, continuing on and on into the clouds until finally ending—over 13,000 feet above sea level—at the summit of a dormant volcano.

It was my turn to do the laundry, so I took a basket of dirty clothes and set it next to the washing machine. Curious, I looked over on the neighbor's side of the yard. Yes, I saw the hot water trickling up from the ground, the hot vapor rising as the water came in contact with the cool mountain air. It had already flooded most of the neighbor's yard and was entering our side. So this old mountain, this old volcano, is still working, I told myself. Pele is still alive and well under this land, her venerable veins still coursing with liquid rock. I repeated her name with reverence as I looked up the slope of the mammoth volcano, its higher slopes covered with thick clouds. In fact the entire sky was overcast, hinting of rain. Sometimes days would pass with the sky like this and it would never rain.

I had stuffed the washing machine with soiled clothes and was measuring a cup of detergent when I heard a slight hissing coming from behind. I turned and scanned the backyard and found, a few yards up the slope, thin wisps of steam rising. I added the soap to the filling water, closed the lid of the machine and went to investigate.

A small vent had cracked open in the ground, though no water was flowing out. The soil around the fissure was wet and was crumbling into the opening. I didn't remember feeling an earthquake. I squatted there, watching the steam, a bit alarmed and yet in awe. I looked over to the neighbor's yard and saw that the hot water was now seeping under the house. There isn't anything we can do about it, I thought. We can only hope that things don't get worse.

Then a funny, airy thought came to my mind. I began to wonder if it was at all possible to harness this energy of Pele; there'd be enough heat to pass around for several lifetimes. I started thinking of a possible scheme to tap that great source of energy below us, which undoubtedly could supply all of our homes with hot water and electricity. Then I became alarmed by my thoughts. Throughout most of my productive life, I have always tried to be scientific in my outlook on natural phenomena. I have always tried to analyze superstitions as mental chains on everyday people. Yet, through it all, I've never been able to shake off certain superstitions completely. In other words, in this instance, I didn't want to offend Pele by suggesting that her lifeblood be used for commercial purposes.

I don't know why I had suddenly engaged in thoughts of commercialism. I've been anti-establishment, anti-capitalist, anti-pollution, anti-development, anti-this and anti-that for most of my life. I've always had a lot of respect for Pele and her unbridled power. She should be left alone, not raped. Violators beware: if there's one woman who isn't going to take any crap, it's her. I'd rather be dead than be the focus of her wrath. There was a time when I was opposed to the state using her power—"geothermal energy" was the term the state officials had coined—because I strongly believed that no one should tamper with the forces of nature and because my friends—Hawaiian religious activists who worshipped Pele—were adamantly against it.

The back door opened. Camilla came out and leaned on the wooden railing of the porch. She looked at the neighbor's, then at the steam rising from our side. Her eyes were swollen from sleeping too much.

"I forgot to tell you about that," she said matter-of-factly.

"About what?" I asked.

"That."

"Oh. You mean the vent in our yard?" She nodded. "You felt one earthquake last night?"

"No," she said. "But it was like that since Thursday."

"Since Thursday?" Four days ago. "Why you nevah tell me about it then?"

She shrugged her shoulders. She swirled her long graying hair away from the sides of her face. Her hair had been black-black and thick once. A while back. A long time ago. That's what first attracted me: her long, beautiful black hair. "I don't know. I didn't think it was important."

"Anytime the ground crack open is important. What if the volcano all of a sudden blows up?"

She didn't say anything. She gave me a look of indifference, an expression that meant that nothing right now could get her stirred up. She had been feeling this way for a while now, since hearing that her best friend, Pua Vierra, was dying of cancer in her Kaua'i home. "So . . . if the island goes, then we go," she finally said, to balance my pause.

I studied the wet rocks. Deep inside the 'aina, Pele was there, causing all of this. But it isn't her fault, I said to myself. It isn't her fault.

"Had one call from Joe yesterday morning, when you were in town," Camilla said.

"Joe?"

"Yeah, Joe. Joe."

Joe Vierra, Pua's husband.

He was a friend of mine, years back when we were young radicals. I met him after I came back from college on the mainland. I was full of enthusiasm and idealism, ready to go all out with revolution: Workers of the World Unite! It was the early seventies, the already wintering of the sixties. I met Joe before he married Pua, or rather, before he started living with Pua and her two daughters. He and I met while organizing an eviction struggle.

A mainland developer had sent notices to longtime residents of a pineapple plantation camp on O'ahu, ordering them to leave in thirty days; the pineapple company had sold a large tract of their land to the developer who in turn was planning to build a hotel and resort. Joe became the most outspoken organizer of the community, for Joe was very close to his grandparents who had lived in the camp for over fifty years. His grandparents, as well as the rest of the community, did not want to leave. We worked hard and closely together for over a year and became good friends. Then he met Pua and slowly we drifted apart, socially and politically. He turned, more or less, to the reformist route, getting disillusioned with the "high but difficult road to revolution," while I remained staunchly a supporter of the revolutionary proletariat. (Now that I can look back, I must add that our political inclination was more truthful, given the fact that we actually seized power and have been able to maintain this workers' state for over twenty years.) But though we never saw much of each other, we still remained friends. I never stink-mouthed him, and I know he never did that to me. And when he decided to marry Pua, he invited both Camilla and me to their wedding and reception, though we couldn't attend it at the time. We did send them a card, with twenty dollars inside, I believe.

Pua was my wife's friend; they had met while working at a small silicon chip shop in Mililani. Pua wasn't political at first, though she did have strong ideas at the time and was pretty outspoken. It was my wife (my girlfriend at the time) who got her involved in the mainstream of radical politics. Later, though she still agreed with what my wife was saying about the decadent nature of imperialism, she became more involved with IMUA!, an organization of revolutionary Hawaiian activists. IMUA! began organizing a movement to make Molokai, Kaua'i, Ni'ihau and parts of the Big Island a separate revolutionary Hawaiian nation, and Pua became one of their leaders. Though there were political differences, my wife and she still had a lot of unity at the job site, and through it all, they became better friends than Joe and I had become.

"So what Joe from Kaua'i said?" I asked. It was the first time he had called us in almost five years. By the look on Camilla's face, I knew it was something bad.

"He said she's all right. But she's too weak to walk around." Camilla looked up towards the summit. "He told me she only has a few months more," she said softly. "At the most."

"Oh."

"He asked me to come to Kaua'i. Pua has been asking about me and Joe thought it would be good for Pua if I came over there and saw her, stay with them for a week or so."

"Yeah, das a good idea," I said, with a touch of jealousy. "So when you going leave?"

Camilla looked at me with sensitive, soft eyes, knowing that she had touched a soft spot.

She read me well. I read her well. We've been reading each other well for the thirty-seven years we've been together. "So when you going leave?" I repeated. "How long you going stay there?"

She gazed up the slope, then at the hot spring on the neighbor's side. "I don't know. Maybe a week. Maybe a little more. You can manage?"

I nodded my head. "No worry about me," I said. "This old man can survive anything. Even if the mountain blows up and Pele gets angry at me fo' why I nevah give her something fine fo' drink, I can manage. I can survive. I'm a survivor. You know that."

Camilla smiled. Her eyes opened wide and stayed on me and spoke to me; they began tasting me.

I read her eyes well. I glanced up the slopes, at the thick motionless clouds, then followed her into the house.

Camilla needed some things for dinner and I needed to get some screen to replace the old ones on the front of the house. So I got into my truck and drove into town. Though it was early afternoon, it was a cold day and I had put on a flannel shirt; you could see the vapor coming from my mouth, that's how cold it was. I thought about the call from Joe, and I was feeling a little hurt that Joe hadn't extended the invitation to me. A bit hurt. After all, we had gone through a lot of shit together in the early years, and, when you come down to it, it was actually I who introduced Joe to Pua.

As I drove down the road to town, I reminisced about that time. Some radical professor was throwing a party at his North Shore house, and he had invited everyone who called himself or herself a community organizer or radical or communist or revolutionary. That was the time when we were all loosely connected to one another; the polemics weren't mature or understandable or divisive yet; we more or less knew we had differences, but somehow we weren't articulate enough about the issues to get into any major debates. At first Joe didn't want to go. He was a shy guy, although in front of a bunch of people, he could work the crowd well with his grass roots agitation. The workers would listen earnestly to him, he knew what he was talking about; after all, he was from the working class. All of us were somewhat in awe when he spoke; I think some of us were even jealous of his skills. I know I was, to a point, though I later combatted that tendency when I began to realize that whatever it took to move the struggle forward was more important than the accumulation of personal gain. Anyway, I finally persuaded Joey to come with us to the party, and Camilla, my girlfriend then, brought along her friend, Pua. It wasn't an arrangement kind of job at all. Pua needed a ride so we took her there. And she brought along her two small daughters. Well, her two daughters took a liking to Joey; on the long way home, both of them sat on his lap in the back seat, playing with his beard, listening to his stories, later falling asleep in his arms. A week later, Joey moved into Pua's tiny unit in the housing.

I knew Camilla knew I was hurt. That was why she took me in and held my head on her soft, rising chest. She cradled me like a child; when she felt like being cradled, I did the same for her.

I drove to the hardware store first and parked in the front. Dreyfus, the proprietor, greeted me at the door. I asked him where I could find the screen and he directed me to the back of the store, where his teenage helper measured the needed yardage for me. I paid for it at the checkout counter.

"Strange weather we're having, aren't we?" Dreyfus said.

I shrugged my shoulders; no stranger than last week or the week before. He was just trying to make conversation. "Yeah, I guess," I said. Then I thought about the steam and the hot water in the backyard. "Hey Dreyfus, you heard of anyone's yard where the ground's cracked open and steam and hot water start gushing out?"

Dreyfus looked at me with a puzzled look, then shook his head slowly. "No, can't say I have. Why . . . have you?"

I took a deep breath. "Yeah. As a matter of fact, I have something like that happening in my backyard."

"What about your backyard?"

"There're cracks in the ground with hot steam and hot water gushing out. You felt any earthquakes recently?"

"No, not that I know of."

"Yeah, that's what I thought. I didn't feel anything like an earthquake, either. This world's changing so fast."

"You say you got hot water and steam coming out of your backyard?"

I nodded my head.

"Christ, sounds like old Madame Pele is about to have some kind of powwow soon." He chuckled.

I smiled weakly at his bad joke, then told him thanks and goodbye.

I dropped the screen in the bed of my truck and started to walk towards the market. Then I heard someone calling my name from behind. I stopped and turned.

"Eh . . . you Dennis Lim?" I stared at the heavy-set man with medium-length graying hair, wearing faded blue jeans and boots and a flannel shirt with a sleeveless jacket over it. He was maybe a few years younger than me. He looked like he had gone hunting, or was about to go. I studied his face, and though he looked familiar, I could not place him or remember his name.

"You Dennis Lim, right?"

"Yeah . . . that's me. I know you?" I approached him, stopped a step away from him. We shook hands.

"Renardo José. You remember me?"

A smile came to my face. "Rennie José? From Kanewai?"

He smiled, nodding his head. "Yeah, das me."

He and his older brother and I used to run around together when we were kids. We were neighbors, living a couple houses away from each other. A long time ago.

"Eh brah! So how you been?" I said. I shook his hand again, this time vigorously. "Eh, goddamn! It's been so long since I last saw you. What . . . twenty years? Thirty years? Something like that?"

"Something like that."

"So what you doing here?"

"Hunting." He nodded his head in the direction of the mountain.

"What—by yo'self?"

"No-no. With my friend. We jus' came back down from the slopes. Bagged one hundred-pounder."

"Eh . . . you looking good."

"You too."

"So what you doing now?"

"Oh, jus' waiting fo' my friend come back out. He went inside get somet'ing fo' grind."

"Eh, come over my house. I live only a few miles down the road. My wife can make up something good real fast."

He smiled appreciatively, shaking his head. "Nah, brah. I no like make imposition. Anyway, my partner and me we have to go back to the hotel and wash up. Our flight leaves tonight."

"Back to Honolulu?"

He nodded his head.

"Eh, c'mon. Bring yo' friend, too. Come over the house. My wife can make one fast dinner. In fact, I going to the market right now for her, I gotta buy some things for her. Come . . . come over and drink a few with me. We can talk about the old days."

He laughed lightly. "No, brah. Wish I could, but cannot. We gotta make tracks back to the hotel and get ready. But mahalos anyway. So how long you been living here?"

"About seven years. And you? Where you living now?"

"Kanewai. Same place. Still yet."

"How's the place . . . still the same?"

"Still the same. Ho . . . there's my friend coming outta the market. Okay, brah." We shook hands again. "Good to see you after all these years. And mahalos again fo' the invites. Maybe next time."

"Yeah, brah. Maybe next time. Drop in next time. My number not in the phone book, but you can ask anybody in town where I stay and they going tell you. The place small here. Everybody know everybody else."

"Okay, brah," he said, shaking my hand again, then walking off towards their rented four-wheel drive.

"Okay, brah," I said, stunned by the quickness of our meeting.

We had been tight together when we were in high school. Then I went off to a mainland college on a scholarship. His older brother had gotten drafted into the army, and Rennie followed him a couple years later, both sent to Vietnam. Sonny never came back. I met up with Rennie after he was discharged and I was pau with college. I left college hating it and most of the people there; I was raring to go back to my old friends, to immerse myself again in my proletarian roots. Coincidentally, both of us were into dope: he got into the habit while in Nam and I got it while in college. He became the neighborhood dealer and he used to turn me on all the time, and once in a while I used to help him unload his stuff to my downtown connections. Then he got burned in a bad deal, and he kind of blamed me for it, though he never said anything to me directly, since I had connected him with this guy from town whom I knew only casually. He just didn't talk to me after that. Our friendship just fell apart. A year later, after I had given up dope and was getting heavy into radical politics, I heard from his youngest brother that he had been busted and sent to prison. And that was the last I heard of him. Until seeing him now in front of the shoe store.

I watched Rennie get in, and as his friend drove off, he waved at me. I waved back. Then I shouted, "Say hello to the family!"

Rennie nodded his head and waved again as the vehicle headed down the road.

I stood there for a long minute, thinking about Rennie and

his brother, about Kanewai, and then about Joey and Pua. It was all a long while ago. A long while. Slowly, I got myself going to the market; I just didn't want to slip out of the nostalgia.

After dinner, I went out to the back slope. It was cold, so I wore a thick jacket that I hadn't used for a quite a while. It was a jacket I used in my college days in New York, and it still fit me perfectly.

I sat high above the vents. The steam was rising in trails of white mist, like ghosts leaving the land now that the sun had set. Only thing, there had been no sun the entire day. Then I became aware of the vastness and emptiness of the space around me. I became uneasy. Here I was sitting on this cold, massive mountain and with that huge, endless black sky above. I thought I felt Pele's breath on the back of my neck. I thought I heard her laughing.

I looked down at the house; only the bathroom light on our side of the duplex was on. Camilla taking a shower. Our neighbors were gone. In fact, they had been gone for at least a week now. We didn't know what happened to them. Just one day disappearing. Maybe they had taken a trip, though they always told us if they were going anywhere for a long period of time. But we weren't that concerned because the newspaper boy said that they had cancelled their subscription. Still, we thought it was odd. They were retirees, too; he had taught at the university—geography, I think—and she had been a meteorologist with the former federal government.

The light in the bathroom went off. Now the house melded with the darkness. Leaves and grass rustled behind me, around me; I became aware of everything moving. At first, I became anxious. I was afraid to look behind, thinking that I'd see Pele. I became afraid that the ground beneath me would suddenly explode in a cataclysmic force, blowing me up into bits and bits of insignificant dust. I became colder as the wind became brisker. I wanted to retreat to the house, but my body refused to move.

Then the porch light came on. Camilla came out clutching her nightgown, looking with consternation into the darkness that now hedged the house. She called for me in a tiny voice. I waited a few moments before answering. She chided me for staying out in the cold and told me to come in, that she didn't want to be left alone in the house. She went back in, leaving the light on.

I got up slowly, then anxiously looked behind. I was relieved to see only a black void that could have been inches or a hundred miles away from my face.

I hiked down the slope, stopping for a moment at the steam vent to warm myself, then entered the house, turning off the outside light.

The GARDEN of JIRO TANAKA

After serving over thirty-eight years as a park keeper for the City and County of Honolulu, Jiro Tanaka graciously retired with the feeling that now he could enjoy life at his own leisure. At the small retirement party his co-workers held for him at the park pavilion, Jiro was given gifts and much praise from everyone. His friends asked him how he was planning to spend his retirement years. He smiled softly while scratching the back of his head. "Now I going do dah things I feel like doing," he said.

"So what is it you going do?" they asked.

"Oh, I get plenty things to do. My yardwork. Make trouble fo' my wife. Do nothing." He laughed warmly.

Everyone laughed with Jiro.

Jiro scratched his head again. "Now I can go play wit' my grandchildren any time."

"Jiro—you grandfather? Eh, congratulations!"

Jiro was embarrassed. He smiled. "No . . . I no have grandchildren. Not yet. Maybe soon, but."

The government gave him a comfortable retirement check every other week and free medical and dental benefits and a bus pass for the rest of his life. He often counted the blessings given to him as reward for diligently working the number of years he had for the City and County. The mortgage on his modest home was paid off; he had a wonderful, caring wife; and his only son was grown and enjoying a happy—though childless—marriage. Everything seemed to be taken care of, and sometimes as he lay in the darkness drifting off to sleep, Jiro would feel a mild sense of satisfaction and contentment with how favorably his life had turned out.

He woke up at four one morning—a habit he had followed like a religion for most of his adult life—and went to the bathroom to wash and shave. In the water-spotted mirror he saw himself for the first time in all those years: a tired old man near the end of a comfortable yet uneventful and meaningless life. He stood there stunned, not knowing what to think, gazing at his shallow image: bleary-eyed, face swollen from sleep, short wet white hair standing on end.

Later, over a steaming cup of black coffee and with a lit but unsmoked cigarette between his fingers, he wondered how it was possible that over six decades of his life had passed by so fast. It was as if he had winked a couple of times and life had become a liar and painted him an old man with thin white hair and deep wrinkles etched on his leathery face. He left the morning paper unfolded but unread on the kitchen table for the first time in all those years.

The next morning he woke and sat up at the edge of his bed, staring blankly into the darkness. He began to rise, but changed his mind and sat back down. His joints were cold and stiff and they ached. He lay back in his bed and covered himself with the blanket. Every morning his old bones were a discomfort to him. But this time the little aches and pains were a good excuse for him to stay in bed and not have the bathroom mirror brutally remind him of those lost years of his life.

With his eyes open to the morning darkness, he listened to the sounds of the old house: the shifting of the old oak floor boards, the venetian blinds softly tapping against the windows, the reliable purring of the old refrigerator down the short hall in the kitchen, the delicate humming of the electric clock. Then he tuned his ears to the warm silence that permeated the rest of the house. The sounds he heard were now like punctuation marks, devices that gave the silence time and depth and finiteness.

The sudden buzz of the alarm clock jarred him from his meditation. His wife Hazel stirred awake. She fumbled for the clock and switched the alarm off, then rose methodically off her squeaky bed. Jiro heard the tracking of her house slippers as they flip-flopped flatly on the wooden floor. He listened to the flushing of the toilet, the whining and gurgling of the ancient plumbing coming back to life. Finally, Hazel's footsteps shuffled out the bathroom to the hall where they stopped.

"Jiro? Jiro?" Hazel called out in an alarmed whisper. "You awake?"

He had not heard her come into the bedroom. He lay in silence for a few moments, resenting the fact that his privacy had been disturbed. "Yeah-yeah," he said finally. "I awake."

"Jiro—how come you still in bed? You sick? You not feeling good?"

"No, I all right. I feel like staying in bed fo' little while. Das all."

Hazel groped for the hallway light switch and turned the light on. The naked bulb radiated harshly into Jiro's eyes.

"Why you turn dah light on fo'?" he complained. "Not'ing wrong wit' me."

"Den how come you not awake?"

"I stay awake. You jus' wake me up."

"But how come you not reading yo' pepah, drinking yo' coffee?"

"Cause I feel like staying in bed. Whas wrong wit' dat?" He paused, taking a deep breath to calm himself. "I retired, no? I can do what I feel like doing."

"I know but you always up so early. How come now? You sure you not coming down wit' one cold?"

"Yeah-yeah! I feel all right! I feel like staying in bed. Why you bugging me fo'?"

Hazel stood silent. "No need yell at me," she said painfully. "You no have to yell at me." She flicked off the light and shuffled towards the kitchen.

"I t'ink I going down dah park today," he said to Hazel over a

The GARDEN of JIRO TANAKA **169**

cup of coffee. For the most part, their breakfast together had been silent and tense. "I go see Kazuo and Fortunato . . . go talk story wit' dem guys."

Hazel nodded her head, turning the corners of her mouth.

"Maybe I ask dem if dey need help. Can help dem clean up dah park. Not'ing to do ovah here since I retire."

"You can work on yo' own yard," Hazel said bluntly.

"I do. You nevah see how much dah yard stay so clean since I stay home? Yesterday I wen cut dah grass, dah other day I wen weed dah garden."

Hazel turned her dark eyes away from him, sipping her coffee sullenly.

"Be good to see dem guys," Jiro murmured.

Hazel went to the kitchen sink, taking her dishes with her. She rinsed off the dishes and washed her hands. "Bobby wen call yesterday," she said, while looking out the window and wiping her hands on a dishcloth. The sky was brightening with the morning sun. "He said Laurie went to dah doctor." She paused. "He said dah doctor tol' her she no can have babies. Something wrong inside."

Jiro was still for a long moment, then took a drag from his cigarette. "Whas wrong wit' her?" he asked, smoke streaming from his nostrils.

Hazel shook her head. "I dunno what dah doctor wen tell her. But maybe . . . but maybe dey can adopt one baby."

Jiro shook his head slowly.

"Maybe," Hazel said. "But Bobby said dey going try one 'nother doctor. Fo' second opinion."

"Better if dey get dey own baby." He sighed, glancing at the wall clock. "I going down dah park," he said.

Trash was piled high on every rubbish can, as if nobody had emptied them for weeks. The grass had grown tall and wild, and as Jiro passed the public restrooms, he crinkled his nose because of the stench. He approached a young park keeper, a new face for Jiro, who was adjusting a sprinkler head. "You know where Kazuo or Fortunato stay?" he asked with a smile.

The young park keeper's eyes were red and vapid, he gave Jiro a look of indifference. Then he nodded his head in the direction of the maintenance room where the park equipment was stored. Jiro found Fortunato there, sitting on a stool and sharpening a sickle.

"Jiro!" Fortunato stood up, his face lighting up, his white-white teeth gleaming in the dim room. "You looking good! Good to see you. So dah retirement life good den, eh?"

Jiro nodded his head resolutely. They shook hands. "Is okay. Good change jus' stay home and no do not'ing." He chuckled. "Eh, no mind me asking," looking out the door, "but what happening over here? Ho . . . jus' like nobody taking care dah grounds." He laughed uncomfortably.

Fortunato's smile faded. "I do my best," he said. "But dah young guys . . . dey no geev one shit."

Jiro nodded his head. "I see dey wen hire one new guy."

"Three new guys. But dey always running away, hiding someplace."

Jiro shook his head.

"Young kids," Fortunato continued. "Dey no like listen to dah old-timers. Dey t'ink dey know it all, dem buggahs. Dey like do ev'rything dey own way." He used the sickle to point out the door. "Look out dere. One big mess. Dem buggahs, dey go hide and smoke dey pakalolo allatime." He laughed uneasily. "I tell you, Jiro, nowdays, not like befo'. Ev'rything change. Not like befo'."

Jiro nodded his head. "So where Kazuo?" Jiro asked.

Fortunato's eyes widened with pain. "You nevah hear?"

"Hear what?"

"You nevah hear what happened to Kazuo?" Fortunato shook his head. "Last week he had one stroke. Right on dah baseball diamond, by home plate. Lucky thing I was close by. I was dah only one around. Dah new boys was in dah bushes smokin' dey grass."

"Kazuo? Stroke?" Jiro's voice cracked. "How him? He okay?"

"He in dah hospital. Half his body paralyze."

"Oh no! And he was going retire in little while." Jiro shook his head. "Ho . . . I feel so bad fo' him. Fo' his wife."

They were silent for a long moment, the air in the room suddenly becoming heavy with gloom.

"And so how long he gotta stay in dah hospital?" Jiro asked.

"Fortunato shrugged his thin shoulders. "Dat, I dunno, Jiro."

"Where he stay? What hospital?"

"St. Anselm's. Intensive care."

"I go visit him today."

"I dunno yet if dey allow him visitors."

Jiro looked out the door. "I go ask. I call dem up." He turned to Fortunato. "And his wife? How she taking it?"

Again, Fortunato shrugged his shoulders. "I dunno, Jiro. Not too good, I t'ink."

They were silent again.

"Ah . . . but Kazuo he strong like one ox," Fortunato said finally. "He going recovah fast. No time he going be up and around."

"Yeah-yeah. But still . . . not going be dah same."

Fortunato nodded his head. "Yeah. Not going be dah same."

The two friends talked for a short while longer. Then Jiro bid his friend goodbye, promising to come back again.

Several nights later, in a dream, he planted a large brown seed in his garden. The seed sprouted before his eyes and grew fast into a thick, crawling vine. Yellow flowers bloomed everywhere. Then, from the flowers, oozed children. Dozens of children. And they were smiling and humming a strange melancholy melody. They jumped about and danced circles around Jiro, then ran off with their sing-song voices trailing behind, ringing in Jiro's ears. He ran after them with arms spread, in a desperate need to embrace them, but the vine roped his ankles and he fell face down. Helplessly, he watched the children run off and disappear.

When Jiro woke up that morning, he forgot what he had dreamed. He went about his daily morning routine and, while reluctantly looking at himself in the mirror, was surprised to see his whiskers in a new way. Smiling and delighted at the discovery, he decided against shaving.

"You look terrible," his wife complained at the breakfast table, but all he did was grin and drink his coffee and smoke his cigarettes.

In a few days, Jiro raised a straggly but healthy white growth on his face.

"You look like one old goat," Hazel said. But he just laughed with a boyish disregard, his dark eyebrows raising in jest. "Jiro, you embarrass me. I no like people see me wit' you in public."

Jiro laughed deliriously, frightening Hazel, chasing her out of the kitchen.

After breakfast, he went to work in his vegetable garden and discovered a small weed struggling between two heads of maturing Manoa lettuce. It was a common weed. His garden had been infested with a variety of weeds a while ago and he had waged a bitter war against them. It was a war he thought successful until now. He bent down to pull it out when suddenly he became awed by the weed's simplistic beauty. Never before had he regarded a weed in this way. Gently he touched the shoot, examining closely the fine lines of the leaf. The weed moved him so that he decided to let it be. He yanked out the two Manoa lettuces, then watered the shoot.

Soon weeds sprouted all over the yard. Jiro was elated.

"Jiro! What happening to you?" Hazel asked with alarm. They were eating breakfast in the kitchen. She was aware of the yard going to pot, the wild growth on his face, but had not said anything for a long time until that morning when she just could not hold it in anymore. The weeds had practically taken over the yard, the grass was knee-high.

"Dah yard look terrible, Jiro, jus' like yo' beard. Dah neighbors . . . dey talking 'bout you. I can hear dem talking behind our backs."

"So! Let dem talk 'bout me. Why should dat bother me? Is none of dey business anyway. All dey are is good-fo'-not'ing, lazy nosey buggahs!"

"But Jiro! What happening to you? What kind person you turning out? What kind grandfather you going be?"

Puzzled, he looked into Hazel's worried face. "What you

mean? I not one grandfather."

Hazel dropped her hands into her lap. "Bobby called last night. He said dey adopting one baby, from Korea." She searched Jiro's face for a positive reaction; there was none. "Dah pepahs went through already. Dah baby coming anytime now."

Jiro brooded over the idea of being a grandfather. A smile slowly came to his face. "I going be one good grandfather," he said softly, his eyes twinkling. He stroked his beard. Then he clapped his hands loudly, rubbing them together. "Den I going be one good grandfather! I teach my new grandchild all I can how live one good life. Ho-ho!"

"But not wit' yo' beard. You going scratch dah baby's face. And how yo' grandchild can play in one yard full of weeds?"

Jiro threw his head back, laughing heartily. He had not laughed like that for a long time. Suddenly he was back in his boyhood days, plantation days, swimming naked with school friends in an irrigation ditch. "Jimmy! We go swim down dah ditch! Come on! We go!"

Hazel looked at Jiro with caution. "Jiro . . . what you said?"

"Come on—hurry up!" Jiro insisted. "Bumbye dah big luna he come and catch us!"

The weeds thrived. They had taken over the vegetable garden and were spreading into Hazel's flower bed. Hazel worked furiously to get rid of them, and though she hinted that she would start digging up the rest of the yard, she dared not touch her husband's weeds.

Every night since the first night, without fail, Jiro dreamt of the children. They danced circles around him and sang their sad song, laughing and smiling, but they would never let him come near. The moment Jiro reached to touch them, the children would run off and disappear. And, also without fail, the moment he'd wake the dream would be forgotten.

Jiro's backyard became a miniature forest. In one corner was a grove of haole koa and in another tall buffalo grass. The squat house stood out starkly like a white mushroom on the fringes of a dark, quiet forest. Hazel had stopped talking to Jiro, and most of her time was now spent at Bobby's house with the new baby, she being afraid to bring the baby to their house. Jiro filled the silence by humming a song he had never heard before.

Must be my father's village, Jiro told himself in his dream. Long skeins of fishing nets hung in arches on wooden supports. The roofs of the cottages melded together. He saw the children, their moon-shaped faces with rosy cheeks peeking out of the doorways. He sang their song. Cautiously, they came out, smiling. They began to sing with Jiro. Jiro took a step forward. The children stopped. They ran back into their huts.

While tending to his garden of weeds one afternoon, Jiro heard melodic strains coming from behind the buffalo grass. He straightened up—accidentally dropping a coffee can of chicken manure—and directed his ears to the strange music. It was the song he hummed incessantly to himself throughout the day, the song that played in his mind at nights, lullabying him to sleep. Fear swept through him, making his heart tremble; perspiration flowed from his face. As if possessed by a hypnotic power, he plodded through the bush towards the music, his legs and arms moving stiffly, as if reluctant to go.

He came to a small clearing where the music had taken a reedy timbre and was the loudest. In the middle of the clearing was a tall, thick-trunked plant with large oval leaves. Small rotund fruits, smooth and shiny like tomatoes, hung from the tips of many branches, some fruits a creamy green color, some with a splash of yellow on green, one fruit ripened to a brilliant orange. The music was from the plant, its leaves vibrating with a warm gentle breeze.

He had never seen such a beautiful plant before. He sat on the ground, his eyes fixed on the plant. He touched the ripened fruit, and it broke off cleanly into the palm of his hand. It was soft and cool and had the smell of the ocean.

He fondled the fruit, then bit it. It was crunchy but bitter. Yet he was compelled to eat it all, not knowing why. When he finished, he was left with a large seed, which he dropped at the base of the plant.

The fruit had an immediate soporific effect. His eyes lost their attentiveness and his body began to sway heavily, like a ship listing. Slowly, he got up and lumbered out of the bush, covering the path behind. He entered the house and fell asleep before his head could touch the creases of his pillow.

The children peered from doorways. Jiro took a breath of air, calming himself, then began singing the song. The children inched out. Surprisingly, they came next to Jiro and let him touch their fine, smooth hair. They hedged around him, their dark brown eyes begging him to tell a story. So he did. And they smiled, then laughed. And when he finished telling the story, their eyes asked for more. Happily, he began another.

Everyday he went to the plant, not understanding what this obsession was that was making him eat a bitter fruit daily. And every night he dreamed of the children. He played with them, sang songs with them, told stories. He let them run their thin cold fingers through his beard. He carried them on his back. And he burrowed his nose into their salty childrensmell, closing his eyes and wishing never to lose that smell, though even in the dream he understood that he would never remember any of it when he woke.

Then, one night, he had no dream of the children. Instead, he had a nightmare of the fishing village being belted by a storm of waves as high as a mountain. And he woke up in the cold early morning with his body trembling, his mind swimming madly between the nightmare—the only dream he remembered—and the surrounding cold darkness. And for an unknown reason, he became worried.

He got out of bed. Taking a flashlight from a kitchen drawer, he ran out into the garden, tripped on a hoe and fell face down, the flashlight spinning and rolling away into the bush. He got up, picked up the flashlight, and fought his way through the bush to the clearing. And there he saw—collapsed into a heap of wilted leaves and stems—the plant.

He ran out of the bush and returned with a bucket of water and a handful of manure, sprinkling the fertilizer over the plant and dousing it with water. But it was of no use. He fell to the ground and cried until his tears bled dry. He went back to the house but returned teary-eyed to the clearing several times in the course of the day, hoping to find the dying plant miraculously recovered or to discover that it all had been just a bad dream.

He could not sleep that night, tossing and turning in bed endlessly. Whenever he closed his eyes he saw the horror of the village being lunged at by a stormy sea of monstrous waves.

Before dawn it began to rain. And through the fall of the rain, he heard laughter. A chorus of shrill laughter. And who was laughing and what was the laughter about? Cautiously he got out of bed and put on a jacket, took the flashlight from the kitchen again and went outside. He pushed through the bush to the clearing and shined the flashlight left to right, down to the heap of dead wet leaves, then up at the bombardment of tiny falling raindrops caught in his trembling beam of light. He could not see who was laughing, though it was here that the laughter was coming out the loudest.

He stepped on something sharp and found the ground covered with broken shells of the seeds he had left.

And among the broken seeds were the children.

They were the size of his thumb. They were wet and naked and rolling playfully all over the ground, their blushing skins picking up the dirt.

Carefully Jiro sat down, crossing his legs. He watched the children for a long time, a smile coming to his face. Then, nodding his head in time with their song, he spread his arms to receive them into his warmth and protection.

ABOUT *the* AUTHOR

Gary Pak lives in Kaneʻohe with his wife, three kids and the family dog. On weekends you may find him with most of the above at some soccer field, basketball court or baseball diamond, watching and cheering on his children and the other children of Kaneʻohe.